INITIATION

"Miss Kate Devine," Carole began ceremoniously. "It is my great honor to invite you to join The Saddle Club—to have all the privileges of membership in our great organization."

In the moonlight, the girls could see that Kate was smiling. "Oh, how wonderful!" she said. "I accept, of course!"

"We knew you would," Stevie said. "So we even brought you a horse's head pin."

It was identical to the ones Lisa and Stevie and Carole wore.

"It's beautiful," Kate said.

"Here's to The Saddle Club," Carole announced, putting her hand up in the air. Her friends joined her, clapping hands together.

THE SADDLE CLUB

DUDE RANCH

BONNIE BRYANT

A SKYLARK BOOK
NEW YORK • TORONTO • LONDON • SYDNEY • AUCKLAND

RL 5, 009–012

DUDE RANCH
A Bantam Skylark Book / August 1989

Skylark Books is a registered trademark of Bantam Books, a division of Bantam
Doubleday Dell Publishing Group, Inc. Registered in U.S. Patent and Trademark
Office and elsewhere.

"The Saddle Club" is a registered trademark of Bonnie Bryant Hiller.
The Saddle Club design / logo, which consists of a riding crop and a riding hat,
is a trademark of Bantam Books.

"USPC" and "Pony Club" are registered trademarks of
the United States Pony Clubs, Inc., at The Kentucky
Horse Park, 4071 Iron Works Pike, Lexington, KY 40511-8462

ISBN 0-553-15728-0

Published simultaneously in the United States and Canada

Bantam Books are published by Bantam Books, a division of Bantam Doubleday
Dell Publishing Group, Inc. Its trademark, consisting of the words "Bantam
Books" and the portrayal of a rooster, is Registered in U.S. Patent and Trademark
Office and in other countries. Marca Registrada. Bantam Books, 1540 Broadway,
New York, New York 10036.

PRINTED IN THE UNITED STATES OF AMERICA

OPM   15   14   13

This book is dedicated
to the memory of Marjorie Brown
and to her mother,
my expert, Mel Roemisch.

STEVIE LAKE LIKED to look out on the world from between the ears of her horse. She sat tall in her saddle. Comanche shifted his weight comfortably from one side to the other. She patted him reassuringly with her gloved hand.

It was too hot to wear gloves. The bright Virginia sunshine beat down on Stevie and all of the other riders and horses from the stable's summer-camp program. Stevie was between her two best friends, Carole Hanson and Lisa Atwood. Like Stevie, they were dressed in formal riding habits, sitting stiffly in their saddles.

In front of the line of riders stood Max Regnery, owner of Pine Hollow Stables. He had a sheaf of papers in one hand and was standing next to a board full of ribbons. Today was the last day of camp. It was time for awards, and Stevie suspected the only one she was going to get was "Biggest Troublemaker." She sighed to herself. That was the price she had to pay for trying to have fun. The problem was that her idea of fun wasn't always Max's idea of fun.

A deerfly landed on her wrist and tried to take a bite of her. She took a swat at it. Comanche felt the motion in his reins and thought it was a signal to move. He moved. Max glared at them. Stevie tightened up on the reins and Comanche stepped back.

Max was giving out prizes to the young riders first. Since Stevie and her friends were twelve and thirteen, their awards would come later. In the meantime, she had to sit still, and that wasn't her strongest suit.

Stevie glanced over at Carole to her right. Carole's beautiful curly black hair, which usually hung loose around her shoulders, was tightly braided and carefully folded up under her velvet riding hat. Her dark brown eyes stared straight ahead at Max. She looked both comfortable and attentive. Stevie thought that probably came from Carole's father, a colonel in the Marine Corps. Colonel Hanson was always comfortable at attention too.

Carole had been riding horses since she was a very little girl, and she wanted to spend the rest of her life working with horses. Stevie admired Carole's incredible skill at riding. It was as if she'd been born doing it. Stevie thought it was difficult sometimes to tell where the girl ended and the horse began. She giggled, then glanced over at her other friend.

To her left was Lisa Atwood. Lisa was one of the newest riders at the stable. She'd started classes just a few months earlier. She had learned an awful lot in a very short time—and Lisa, Carole, and Stevie had become the best of friends, too. Stevie shook her head, thinking about how different they all were. Lisa was a straight-A student who attacked every project with purpose and confidence. She usually succeeded at them, too.

Today Lisa was wearing a brand-new riding jacket, carefully tailored for her. Her long hair was in a perfect French braid, and her boots had been polished, not by Lisa, but by the shoemaker at the mall. These things mattered a lot to Lisa's mother, who was always very concerned about what was Proper. One of the reasons Stevie liked Lisa so much was that they didn't matter at all to Lisa. It didn't matter to her that her boots were shiny, but if that was the price she had to pay to ride, she'd let her mother have her boots polished.

Stevie, on the other hand, was very disorganized. She was forever starting vast projects and leaving them unfinished. She had polished her own boots for today's ceremonies—or at least she'd polished the right one.

The phone had rung before she'd gotten to her left boot. She hoped Max wouldn't notice. Her own blond hair was in braids, too, but it didn't stay in braids. The slightest breeze loosened strands of it. She knew she must look a mess. She didn't really care.

Although they were very different, the girls had a few things in common. For one, they were all wearing the same pin—a silver horse head, with the wind blowing the horse's mane. That pin meant that they were all members of The Saddle Club, a club they'd made up themselves. The requirements for membership were that all members had to be horse crazy—there was no question that Carole, Lisa, and Stevie shared that—and they had to be willing to help the other members whenever they needed help. That was what their friendship was all about. At that moment, though, Stevie thought the only help any of them needed was to get out of their sweltering riding outfits and into something more appropriate to the day: a swimming pool.

As soon as the ceremonies were over, they'd all un-tack their horses, say good-bye to their friends until classes started again later in the summer, and then Stevie, Lisa, and Carole would head straight for the Lakes' swimming pool. The very thought of it made Stevie smile. Her smile caught Max's eye. He glanced at her suspiciously, thinking she was up to something. She usually was. She tried very hard to look solemn.

Looking solemn wasn't easy for Stevie, especially when she had something nice to think about. Today she was thinking about tomorrow because tomorrow she and her two best friends were going on a trip together. Becuse of some incredible good luck, the girls were going to visit a friend of theirs, Kate Devine. Kate was a championship rider whose parents owned a dude ranch way out west. Not only was it going to be Stevie's first visit to a dude ranch, it would be the first time she'd ever been west of the Mississippi River.

She could imagine the towering Rocky Mountains, the lonesome pines, the Sierra Madre—whatever that was—the cowpokes lumbering along the Santa Fe Trail, the Indians lurking behind sagebrush or whooping and hollering around the circled wagons, gunfights at high noon. Stevie made a funny face and then giggled to herself. It seemed that everything she knew about the West had come from movies. She had the feeling that the real West wasn't exactly the same as the one Hollywood had created, and she suspected there weren't a lot of bad *hombres* hanging around the saloons these days, either.

"Sit up," Carole hissed at her. "He's looking straight at you."

Stevie glanced at Carole and then looked at Max. He *was* looking straight at her. What had she missed, she wondered.

". . . and in the category of dressage, we have one student who has applied herself especially hard and has made great strides this summer. It gives me pleasure to award the dressage ribbon to Miss Stephanie Lake."

That was Stevie. Max was actually giving her an award! She could barely believe it. She thought she'd been sitting in the sun forever for no reason at all.

Stevie slipped her feet out of the stirrups, swung her right leg over the horse's back, and let herself slide down to the ground. Then she led Comanche to the center of the ring, where Max presented her with the bright, shiny blue ribbon. She felt her face flush with joy when Max shook her hand.

"Good work, Stevie," he said.

"Thanks," she told him. Then she and Comanche returned to their place in line. Carole and Lisa were clapping like crazy for her. She grinned at both of them.

Then it was time for the last two awards of the day. One, for the best overall rider, was a cinch to go to Carole. Nobody could come close to her natural ability at riding, and nobody worked harder to improve her skills. Carole was a shoo-in.

"But before we get to the best overall rider, we have one more important category," Max announced. "The rider who wins this category may one day win the best overall because it shows a rider who has a running start—the rider who is most improved. Usually this goes to experienced riders who just hit their stride in learning, but this year, it's going to a new rider—one who came in here without any experience at all and has, in my opinion, learned years worth of riding in a few short months. Congratulations, Miss Lisa Atwood!"

Carole and Stevie couldn't help themselves. They started cheering out loud and clapping for Lisa because she was their friend, and because she deserved it. Shyly, Lisa accepted her ribbon. As she was walking her horse back to the line, Stevie noticed Lisa scanning the audience, looking to see if her mother had come. She was there all right. Stevie even thought she detected a smile on the woman's face.

Although Mrs. Atwood could get very enthusiastic about new riding jackets and shiny boots, she really didn't understand *riding.* She thought it was just something nice girls should know something about. It was clear she wasn't sure what to think about girls who knew a *lot* about it. Stevie felt sorry for Lisa.

She didn't have long to feel sorry, though, because Lisa's award was followed quickly by Carole's. Carole won the best overall rider ribbon and the whole class stood up in their stirrups to give her a standing ovation.

In spite of the awful heat, Stevie thought it was a just-about-perfect day. After all, any day in which all three members of The Saddle Club got blue ribbons was bound to be just about perfect.

Max left the ring, and the riders all dismounted and led their horses back into the stable area.

"Last one in is a rotten egg!" Stevie announced to her friends.

They knew just what she meant. It only took the girls a few minutes to untack the horses and gather up their own belongings from the stable locker area. Stevie's house was a short walk. They ran. They were wearing their suits under their riding clothes, and within seconds, three sets of riding clothes were scattered by the edge of the pool in Stevie's yard.

Nobody was a rotten egg. They all hit the water at the same moment.

"PUT YOUR TRAY *tables and and seat backs in their full upright and locked positions,*" a smooth voice said over the intercom.

"Those are the nicest words I've ever heard," Carole announced. It was the next day, and the three girls were sitting together in a small airplane. They had been traveling for hours. They'd changed planes twice, and they'd nearly gotten lost in the Denver airport. Carole was really glad that her father had asked the flight attendant to keep an eye out for them. They'd almost gotten on a plane bound for Hawaii!

"Does that mean we're really there?" Lisa piped up.

"I guess so," Carole said. "Every plane we've been on has been smaller than the last. If we have to change again, it's going to be a hang glider and I'd rather walk!"

The girls looked around. Their plane was a twenty-seater. Carole was right.

Stevie, sitting by the window, returned her attention to the land below.

"There are cows down there! And horses! Lots of them!"

"Not necessarily just *cows*," Carole reminded her with a grin. "Dairy herds are just *cows*. But this here's roundup country now! Those could be beef cattle."

Stevie giggled, then instantly sobered. "You mean I'm looking at a lot of hamburgers?" she asked.

There was a snort from the seat behind them. The girls turned around to see a boy about eighteen years old. His eyes were sparkling with laughter.

"What's so funny about hamburgers?" Stevie demanded.

"Well, I wouldn't put it that way myself," he drawled.

"Why not?" Stevie asked. "That's what's going to happen to them, isn't it?"

"Shore," he said. "But when you put it that way, everybody'll know right away you're just a bunch of eastern dudes! Out here, we call that stock." With that statement, the young cowboy returned all his attention to his magazine. The girls turned around in their seats and concentrated on the landing.

Within a few minutes, the plane had landed at a small airport nestled in a valley surrounded by rolling green hills. They grabbed their hand luggage and headed for the steps that took them to the hot tarmac runway.

"*Look!*" Lisa said breathlessly as she stepped onto the ground. Stevie and Carole looked where she was pointing. Beyond the gentle hills that encircled them were the majestic peaks of the Rocky Mountains, still covered with snow in the middle of the summer.

"I think somebody painted those on, don't you?" Stevie asked. The girls agreed that it seemed impossible that something so beautiful could be right there.

"Looks like a postcard," Carole said.

There was another snort, now familiar to the girls. "That's where they put the camera to take the pictures, *dudes,*" the cowboy teased them.

"Hmph," Stevie remarked. She grasped her flight bag and walked purposefully toward the gate. She didn't want to be called a dude any more. After all, it wasn't as if The Saddle Club didn't know anything about riding. Why, they'd won prizes, just yesterday!

"Carole! Stevie! Lisa!"

The girls looked up. There, waving frantically from behind the chain link fence, was their friend, Kate. They ran as fast as their burdens would let them to join her.

It seemed like such a long time since she'd been at Pine Hollow, but their memories of the wonderful fun they'd had with Kate there were vivid. Kate was horse crazy just like they were. She was one of them and the hugs of greeting they all gave one another proved it.

"You look terrific!" Carole said, admiring Kate's new style of clothes. Kate was wearing faded jeans, a red plaid shirt with the sleeves rolled up, soft leather cowboy boots, and a felt hat.

"A little different from the horse-show duds, I guess, but you'll get used to them," Kate told her friends. "Now come on, let's get your bags and head on out to the ranch. We've got a long trip in front of us."

"We just took a long trip," Lisa reminded her.

"That was the *easy* part," Kate said. "This is the *fun* part."

The girls exchanged looks. What was *that* supposed to mean?

"Have you seen Eli?" she asked.

They shook their heads and shrugged. "Who's Eli?" Carole asked in return.

"He's one of our wranglers—a cowboy to you. He was on your flight, but I was so busy looking for you I didn't see him. You could hardly miss him, though. He's eighteen, kind of cute, and speaks with this incredible western drawl—"

"And he makes fun of 'dudes'?" Stevie asked.

"That's the one," Kate said, grinning at Stevie. "I knew you all would get along. One of the ranch's guests drove me and the pickup out here. Eli's driving it back to The Bar None. It's about seventy miles. We can sit in the back of the truck. You can see more that way, but the road's a little bumpy in places, especially the way Eli drives! Hey, there he is now."

Kate introduced the girls to Eli Grimes. He nodded politely at them just as if he'd never met any of them before or made fun of them. Stevie decided that was the best way to handle it, too. She ignored him as well. Without a word, he lugged their suitcases to the pickup truck parked next to the terminal, slung them into the back, took the keys from Kate, got in the truck's cab, and started the motor.

The girls piled into the back of the truck and arranged themselves on the mattresses the Devines kept there for the comfort and safety of their guests.

"Why is it called The Bar None Ranch?" Lisa asked Kate once they'd pulled onto the road.

"Because when my parents first saw it, they knew it was the prettiest ranch they'd ever seen, bar none. Our symbol is an O with a line over it, like this." She traced an $\overline{O}$ in the dust on the truck bed.

"Neat," Lisa said.

Carole wanted to change the subject to her favorite one: horses and riding. Only instead of Carole being the one with the answers, she was now the one with the questions. Carole was lying on her stomach on the truck bed. She bent her knees and crossed her feet at the ankles.

"Okay, now, let's get down to business. Just how different *is* Western riding?" She propped herself up on her elbows.

Kate leaned back against the cab of the truck, looking completely at home in the Western setting. One arm circled her bent legs, the other rested along the side of the truck. She looked out across the hilly countryside, covered with lush grassland. Across a field to their right, a mare and her foal stood comfortably under a shade tree, munching at the grass.

"Look familiar?" she asked Carole, pointing to the pair of horses.

Carole smiled. "Sure, it reminds me of Delilah and Samson." Delilah was a mare at Pine Hollow and Samson was her foal.

"And how about that one?" Kate asked. She pointed to a gray horse with black dappling.

"That one looks like Pepper," Lisa said. Pepper was the horse she rode most of the time at the stable.

"Right, and that one over there is sure to remind you of Patch," Kate said. "And the horse you ride, Stevie—that's Comanche, right? There's a chestnut in a pasture ahead that looks a lot like him. You won't find any Thoroughbreds or the other fancy horse-show breeds like Holsteiners out here. You will find Quarter

Horses, Arabians, and Appaloosas. Those, especially the Quarter Horses, are good *working* horses. But underneath, they're all horses."

"You mean there aren't *any* differences between English and Western?" Carole asked, wrinkling her brow.

"Well, not exactly," Kate told her. "There are lots of differences. You only hold the reins with one hand, for instance, and when you want to turn, you just lay the rein on the opposite side of the neck. That stuff's easy, though. You'll get used to it right away."

"And if we don't, Eli's going to be there to laugh at us! That's going to make us learn fast!" Stevie said.

"Maybe it will," Kate said. "And maybe there are a few things *Eli* could learn, too."

"Like how to post!" Lisa suggested.

Kate smiled to herself and then began laughing. The girls knew that the very idea of Eli Grimes rising and sitting in the saddle with the beat of the horse's trot was just plain funny. "I don't think you could ever teach a wrangler to post," she said. "But I think you can already sit a trot. So, see? Western's going to be easier for you than English would be for him."

"Oh!" Stevie said after a moment, surprise in her voice. The girls looked where she was looking. Evening was coming and the sky was beginning to darken. The sun, sitting on the crest of the mountains to the west, had streaked the clouds with brilliant shades of pink, red, and purple. "I think this must be where they put the camera for *those* postcards, too," she said, recalling Eli's remark at the airport. "I'm really glad I brought my camera. Does it always look like this?" she asked. She carefully framed her friends against the backdrop of the sunset and snapped a photo.

"Not always," Kate said. "Usually it's prettier. And wait until you see the sun*rise*! It's as pretty as can be and we can see it from the porch of our very own bunkhouse."

"Sunrise? You must be kidding," Lisa said. "No way I'm going to be up early enough to see that!"

"That's what *you* think!" Kate said. "Listen, we'll be at the ranch now in about ten minutes. Mom'll feed us some supper and then we can start planning the things we want to do while you're here."

"Ride," Lisa said.

"Check," Kate said. "We'll be doing plenty of that. We've also got a barbecue planned and a couple of picnics, and we're going to have a roundup this week. That should be neat! Anything else you especially want to do?"

Lisa and Carole were full of suggestions. Carole wanted to learn about breaking in horses. Lisa was interested in swimming and mountain riding.

As they chatted, Stevie felt a small pang. There *was* one sour note to this trip, but she didn't want to make a big deal of it. It was that her thirteenth birthday was coming up in just a week. Birthdays were always very special to her, particularly since she shared them with her twin brother, Alex. He could be a bore and a nuisance 364 days a year, but on their birthday, he was her *brother*. Their parents always made a fuss about it. The twins usually had a poolside party with a cookout. Stevie would miss that this year, a lot. Still, she was determined not to upset anybody else with her own problem. She'd just have to miss it this year. And she was lucky to be on such a neat trip. There would be lots of other years, lots of opportunities to have birthday parties. It wouldn't matter at all. Much. She abandoned her lonely thoughts and listened to her friends talking once again.

"So there is a swimming pool?" Lisa asked eagerly.

"Not a pool. A hole. It's a place where the beavers dammed up the river and there's a nice deep swimming spot."

"Are there still real beavers there?"

"Somebody's got to be sure the dam's in working order!" Kate said. But don't worry—they spend most of their time underwater. You probably won't see them. Of course, you may feel one with your feet. You'll know it by the soft fur and—"

"Don't listen to her," Carole said as Lisa shuddered. "She's been spending too much time with Eli."

Lisa nodded. "And if she teases us 'dudes' too much, we won't give her her present, will we?"

"What present?" Kate asked, suddenly very interested.

"Tell us the truth about the beavers," Carole said.

"I've never seen one. Or felt one," she said. "And that's the truth."

"Okay, we'll give you your present. In the bunkhouse."

The pickup truck pulled off the two-lane highway it had been following since leaving the airport. The road was now a rutted dirt path. First they drove through a stand of trees that bordered a creek. "Swimming hole's that way," Kate announced, pointing to the right. The road wound around a hill. On either side, there were pastures, enclosed by wooden post fences.

"We're on our property now," Kate said. "Those cattle over there belong to Bar None. And here's home."

The truck drew to a stop in front of a sprawling ranch house with a wooden porch. It looked like it belonged on a postcard, too. There was a barn behind the house and there were a number of smaller cabins circling the main house. Stevie suspected they were the guesthouses, or bunkhouses.

"Look, there's even a triangle by the door. Don't tell me that's how your mom calls everybody in for lunch!" Stevie said.

"Nope. I get to ring it! You can have turns, too. Maybe," Kate joked.

Eli dropped the tailgate of the truck and helped the girls down. Kate's parents appeared on the porch and welcomed the girls warmly.

"Colonel and Mrs. Devine, it's *great* to be here!" Carole bubbled.

"Well, it's great to have you here," Kate's mother said. "All of you. But we have one firm rule here on the ranch and that is no last names. Everybody calls us Phyllis and Frank. Now come on in and have some supper. I'll have the wranglers put your bags in your bunkhouse. You all must be exhausted from your long trip."

"Plum tuckered out," Lisa said, nodding sagely. Her friends broke into laughter at her use of the un-Lisa-like expression.

"I think she's been watching too many cowboy movies," Stevie said, poking her.

Lisa grinned. "If we're about to eat, can I ring the triangle?"

"You could," Phyllis agreed. "But since everybody else has already *had* supper, you might confuse everyone. Why don't you wait until morning? Breakfast is served at six-thirty on the dot. You can ring it then."

Lisa stifled a yawn. "I think, under the circumstances, that I'll wait until lunch to ring it, okay?"

"No problem," Phyllis said.

The girls followed her inside to the dinner table, where a rich and filling stew awaited them. The girls were both hungry and tired. The Devines talked with Carole, catching up on her family news. Carole knew them originally because her father and Frank had been in the Marine Corps together for many years. They had a lot of friends in common. Now, Colonel Devine was retired, but he still wanted to know about his old friends.

After dinner, the girls helped clear the table and then stumbled across the yard to their bunkhouse. The four girls were being housed in a small building with two rooms. Kate pointed out the bedroom with two sets of bunk beds. "That's why we call it a bunkhouse," Kate told them. There was also a small sitting room and a bathroom. And they had their own little porch, complete with rocking chairs.

"This is neat!" Lisa announced as she peered around the place.

"Neat enough that I've earned my present?" Kate asked, reminding the girls of their promise to her.

"You earned your present a long time ago," Carole assured her. "I think it's time for a Saddle Club meeting—pajama-party style."

The girls all donned their pajamas and gathered on the porch of their bunkhouse. They put their chairs in a circle. The night air was cool and fresh. Beyond the roof of the porch, a sky full of stars glimmered in the velvet black night, and a three-quarter moon cast a pale light on the ranch. Crickets chirped in the grass. The girls heard the comforting sound of a horse's whinny in a nearby corral.

Lisa and Stevie looked to Carole to do the talking. "Miss Kate Devine," she began ceremoniously. "It is my great honor to invite you to join The Saddle Club—to have all the privileges of membership in our great organization."

In the moonlight, the girls could see that Kate was smiling. "Oh, how wonderful!" she said. "I accept, of course!"

"We knew you would," Stevie said. "So we even brought you a horse head pin."

Lisa took a package out of her bathrobe pocket and handed it to Kate. Kate opened the tissue and looked at her pin. It was identical to the ones Lisa and Stevie and Carole wore.

"It's beautiful," Kate said. "It looks just like a horse I once rode in a show. Her name was Crescent because of a marking on her flank."

"Did you take a ribbon with her?" Lisa asked.

"A blue," Kate said, remembering. "I took a lot of blue ribbons when I was riding in shows, actually. They're all in a cabinet in my room. But this means more to me." She looked at her pin. "It's not going in any cabinet. I'm going to wear it!"

"Here's to The Saddle Club," Carole announced, putting her hand up in the air. Her friends joined her, clapping hands together.

"Now the next Saddle Club activity is going to be a good night's sleep," Lisa said sensibly. "Is breakfast *really* at six-thirty?" she asked Kate.

Kate nodded. "Really," she said.

3

"RISE AND SHINE!" Kate Devine's voice broke through the hazy mist of Stevie's dream. "Sun's up—time for you to be up too! Breakfast will be served in five minutes. Lisa, it's almost time to ring the bell!"

"You *must* be kidding!" Stevie groaned. "Are you actually standing there being *cheerful* at six-thirty in the morning?"

"Bingo! You win the prize," Kate said. "And besides, I'm *always* cheerful at six-thirty."

"So am I," Carole said, sitting up in her upper bunk. "But that's because I'm always sound asleep then, too."

There was a loud thump as Lisa's bare feet hit the floor of the bunkhouse. She was up, and from the surprised look on her face, very much awake.

23

"Somebody lead me to my toothbrush," Stevie groaned.

In the end, it only took the girls a few minutes to don their shirts, jeans, and boots and emerge from their bunkhouse, ready for breakfast.

The sun was up, though still low on the eastern horizon. There was a cool freshness in the air. Morning dew sparkled on the grass, and birds chirped in the trees that gave shade to the ranch house.

"I'm glad we're up so early," Carole said.

"All this fresh air and sunshine has gone to your head, huh?" Stevie asked.

"I just can't wait to start riding. What's on for today?" Carole asked Kate.

"Breakfast, then to the corral for a couple of hours, then lunch, then into town to run some errands for my mom and to give you dudes a taste of the *real* West."

"Sounds okay to me, but I wish you'd stop calling us dudes," Stevie complained. "The way some people say it, it sounds like it's an incurable disease." She made a face. She didn't like to be thought of that way, though she knew Kate didn't really agree.

"Don't take Eli too seriously," Kate said, understanding what Stevie was thinking. "And, after all, this *is* a dude ranch."

That was something for Stevie to think about, and she got a look at some of the other visiting dudes as they went into breakfast. The Bar None had about twenty other guests. There were two families, one with four kids, one with five. The kids were much younger than The Saddle Club, which Stevie thought was too bad. Then, there were three couples. One seemed to be on their honeymoon. That was Stevie's guess, anyway, after she saw the husband stumble on the steps because he was too busy gazing into his wife's eyes. The other two couples were much older and appeared to be vacationing together.

Since the girls were going to spend all of their time together, and not on trail rides with the other guests, Stevie didn't pay any more attention to the other people than that. But she *was* glad to know for the Devines' sake that The Bar None had all of its bunkhouses and guest rooms full.

The girls could barely believe the breakfast Phyllis Devine served them. Each of them had a steak, scrambled eggs, sausage, bacon, and fried potatoes.

"What's for dinner?" Carole asked, gazing in amazement at the plate that was put in front of her. "Cocoa Puffs?"

Kate grinned at her. "Dinner will be big too. And you won't believe the appetite you're going to have. Riding horses all day really makes you hungry. You may have trouble this morning because you weren't riding yesterday, but tomorrow you'll be eating like a—a—"

She paused, and Stevie rolled her eyes while Lisa giggled.

Then the wonderful smell of the unusual breakfasts in front of them reached the girls' noses. Much to their own surprise, they dug in. There wasn't much talk in the next few minutes while they ate their Western-style breakfasts. And after they'd cleared their table, it was time to get to the corral.

"Every morning, the wranglers bring the horses in from the pastures where they spend the night," Kate explained as she led the girls to the ranch's outbuildings. "Back east, you usually have to keep them inside for protection or because the stables don't have enough land to let them loose. Our horses here would hardly know what to do in a box stall. They love the freedom of the range. Just watch tonight when we let them loose again," she said.

Following Kate's lead, the girls perched themselves atop the wood-rail fence that surrounded the ranch's corral. From the corral, a single horse could be taken to the saddling area whenever needed. At the moment, there were no horses in the corral at all.

Eli was riding a horse in the pasture where all the horses were grazing. He had a dog with him. While The Saddle Club watched, Eli and his dog rounded up about twenty-five horses, about a third of the total herd, to be used by the guests that day. The dog knew what he was doing, and so did Eli. They worked like a perfect unit, cutting out just the horses Eli wanted, leaving the others, and getting the group headed for the corral.

"Isn't he something?" Kate asked.

Stevie nodded. She had to admit that it was quite a show and she was beginning to understand something about Western riding. It was different from English, but that didn't mean it was easier. When it came to doing that kind of work on a horse, Stevie *was* a dude, and so were her friends, no matter how good they were at riding.

"Come on, let's open the gate for Eli," Kate said, hopping into the corral and running across to the entrance. She unlatched the heavy gate. Then Stevie, Lisa, and Carole helped her swing it open just in time for the arrival of the first of the horses from the pasture. As soon as the last one was in—the horse carrying Eli—the girls shut and latched the gate tight.

"Much obliged," Eli said politely. He dismounted, secured his horse to a fence post, and began the work of assigning horses to riders.

He carefully eyed each of the girls and then, one by one, cut out horses for them. He gave Carole a strawberry roan. That was a chestnut horse with white hairs among the auburn ones. Her horse was named Berry.

Lisa's horse was a bay mare. She was a rich brown color with a black mane and tail and her name was Chocolate.

Kate's horse apparently was the one she always rode. He was an Appaloosa named Spot. She cut him out herself on foot and began saddling him so she'd be able to help her friends.

That left Stevie. Eli scanned the remaining horses. Stevie had a sneaking suspicion he was trying to find an especially difficult horse for her. When he finally chose, she didn't know whether the horse would be difficult, but she certainly knew he was funny-looking. Eli had selected a skewbald horse for Stevie. He had large blotches of white and brown on him, so irregular that Stevie almost laughed. One of the first things a rider learned about horses was that looks didn't matter at all, but in the case of *this* horse, Stevie wondered.

"We call him Stewball," Eli drawled. "He *likes* dudes."

The way he said it made Stevie wonder exactly *how* the horse liked dudes. For breakfast?

There was no way, no way in the world, that she was going to let Eli know she was nervous. She took a deep breath, looked Eli straight in the eye, and asked, "Where's his tack?"

Eli handed the bridle to Stevie. She knew it was a test. He wanted to see if she could put it on the horse.

The bridle was a little different from the ones at Pine Hollow, but it only took her a few seconds to figure it out. She slipped it over Stewball's head and slid the bit into his mouth, adjusted a few of the straps, and smiled triumphantly at Eli. He nodded noncommittally and returned to the barn.

He returned with a saddle for her. That was a little bit more of a challenge. For one thing, it weighed at least twice as much as the English saddles she was used to. For another, it had a lot more parts and the adjustments were different.

When Stevie struggled just to lift the saddle onto Stewball's back, Eli gave her a withering look, took the saddle from her, and finished the job. He also adjusted the stirrups for her. Then he handed her the reins and walked away.

Stevie had the feeling he didn't walk very far, though. She was sure he was just standing a few feet off, waiting to watch her mount. She slid her left foot into the stirrup, lifted herself straight up as Max had taught her, swung her right foot over Stewball's rear, and lowered herself into the saddle, finding the right stirrup with her right foot.

There, she thought to herself. *Let him smirk at that.* But when she turned around, Eli was totally engrossed in helping another of the ranch's guests tack up his horse.

"Come on, girls. Time to hit the trail!" Kate and the others had finished tacking up and were mounted and ready to go. She led the way to the corral's gate. Eli unlatched the gate for them and then clicked it shut behind them. They were ready for their first Western trail ride.

At first, they walked the horses slowly to warm them up and to get accustomed to the differences between Western and English style.

"This really isn't very different at all," Lisa remarked. "I mean, they're just horses and we're just riders, right?"

"That's pretty much the way it goes," Kate said, smiling. "I knew you'd get the hang of it right away. There *are* differences, of course. Like you only hold the reins with one hand. And your stirrups are hung lower so you have more control if you've got a steer on a rope attached to your saddle horn. The horses don't canter, they lope, but it's really the same thing—"

"And we don't post?" Lisa asked.

"Actually, if you want to post, you can," Kate said. "But since the stirrups are long, you won't rise high. You shouldn't need to anyway. Wait until you feel Chocolate's trot. It's smooth as a milk shake."

The thing that seemed the most different to Stevie wasn't the saddle or the horse, but the *place.* "I'm not used to trails like this," she said, pointing to the hills and mountains in front of them.

"Now, that does take some getting used to," Kate agreed. "Our nearest neighbor is about five miles. It's not like that in Virginia, is it?"

"Not at all," Stevie agreed. "But I think I could get to like it." She relaxed in her saddle and enjoyed the ride. Lisa was right. Western riding was just riding, and that was good enough for her.

BY THE TIME the girls got to the town of Two Mile Creek that afternoon, the trail ride was a pleasant memory. Lunch was an even pleasanter one. They couldn't believe how hungry they'd been and how they'd scoffed up the chili that Phyllis had cooked.

"Hope you're not too full for some ice cream," Kate said. "We've got a wonderful little shop here in town. It specializes in sundaes. But of course, if you had too much at lunch—"

"Let's try it," Carole said eagerly. "After all, if we can't finish the sundaes, we can always get doggie bags."

"Out here, we call them dogie bags," Kate said, pronouncing the *o* as in owe. "In case you didn't know it, a dogie is a motherless calf."

"I have the funny feeling we won't have any left-

32

overs, anyway," Carole said, and they all agreed that was true.

Two Mile Creek looked a little like a town in a Western movie, Stevie thought, looking down the main street. Although the street was paved and there were no horses hitched to railings, the wooden side-walks were covered like porches and she was very glad for the shade on the hot summer afternoon. There were a few stores specializing in Western souvenirs, but there were also the usual kinds that would be found in any downtown: three shoe stores, a jewelry store, a fast-food hamburger place, a videotape-rental store, a drugstore, a convenience store, and, best of all, an ice cream parlor. The girls ran the errands for Kate's mother as quickly as possible and then headed for the ice cream parlor.

It was decorated like an old-fashioned sweetshop. It was nothing like the girls' favorite hangout back home, TD's. Instead of booths, there was a long marble coun-ter where the girls sat. Behind it was a vast selection of drink and sundae flavors. Unfortunately, there was also a very large mirror on the wall; Stevie was afraid that if she made a pig of herself, she'd have to watch herself eat every bite. She just ordered a dish of vanilla ice cream.

The girls relaxed over their treats and eagerly chat-ted about their ride that morning.

"See, I told you you'd like Western riding," Kate said. "After all, *I* do. The thing to remember about it is that nothing's there just for show. Western riding is all business. New riders sometimes think that saddle horn is just to hold onto. But that's not true at all. Wait until we have our roundup later this week. You won't be doing much roping, but you'll see Eli do some and you'll see what a pommel is *really* for."

"That'll be neat," Lisa said eagerly. "Will we sleep out, too?"

"Yup. Under the stars, just like in the movies."

"What days will that be?" Stevie asked.

"Oh, I think the roundup will be Wednesday and Thursday. Why? You got a date?"

Saturday was Stevie's birthday. She really didn't think she'd want to be on a trail on her birthday. But she wasn't sure exactly *what* she wanted. "No, I was just wondering," she said.

Carole glanced at Stevie. She could tell something was on her friend's mind, and she thought she knew what it was. "Isn't your birthday coming up soon?" she asked.

"Yeah, it's on Saturday," Stevie answered nonchalantly.

Carole knew from the way she'd responded that *that* was what was on Stevie's mind. Carole had something up her sleeve for Saturday, but she didn't want Stevie to know about it. She just said, "Oh," noncommittally.

Stevie returned her attention to her vanilla ice cream until her whole bowl was empty. So was everybody else's.

Kate glanced at her watch and then at the door. As she did, there was a very loud bang.

Lisa jumped in her seat. "What was *that?*" she asked.

"Let's go see!" Carole said, standing up from the counter. The girls paid for their ice cream and dashed to the door. There had been three more loud bangs just while they were paying.

Stevie could barely believe what she saw when she stepped out onto Two Mile Creek's main street. A crowd of people was gathered around just watching as a disaster was unfolding in front of them!

They were right across the street from the bank. Three cowpokes were backing out of the bank, holding large sacks of money.

"Don't nobody try to follow us!" one of them hollered, brandishing his gun at the crowd. "Ain't gonna spend my life behind bars!"

Three horses were hitched in front of the bank. As the men backed away from the doorway, they unhitched their horses and began to mount. Another shot rang out across the street. This one was louder and turned out to be the report of a rifle. It came from the roof across the street. One of the horses jumped. The rider spun around, dropping to the ground and rolling in the dirt. He aimed his six-shooter at the source of the rifle shot and got off two rounds.

There was a loud shriek of pain. "You'll never get away with this!" the man cried from the roof. Then, as the girls watched, he dropped and rolled off the roof, clutching his side in pain.

The crowd went "Ooooh!"

"Let's get out of here, boys!" one of the robbers said to the others. The three leapt onto their horses and turned to leave town at a gallop. But before they could go, the sheriff and a posse arrived on the far end of the street, completely blocking the way.

The lawmen began shooting at the robbers in an impressive show of strength. It was clear they were shooting to warn, not to kill. The robbers heeded the warning. Before any of the bullets found their mark, the robbers tossed their guns into the street and raised their hands.

The crowd went "Aaaaah!"

"Okay, McClanahan," the sheriff said fiercely. "The game is over. You and your boys have stolen your last payroll. And you'll swing for the murder of Marshall Ellsworth, and for my deputy there." He pointed to where the man had fallen off the roof.

The sheriff neared the robbers and was about to put handcuffs on them when McClanahan reached into his boot and brought out a pistol. "I said you wasn't gonna take me alive and I meant it!"

Then another shot rang out, this time from the roof of the bank. McClanahan dropped down off his horse.

The crowd went "Yaaaaay!" Stevie was just about to get really angry at all these people standing around just *watching* all this bloodshed when she realized suddenly what was going on. It wasn't real at all! It was a show for the tourists—the *dudes*—and she'd been taken in completely. She wouldn't let Eli know about that!

The remaining bank robbers began to flee, but the sheriff and his deputies shot them both before they reached the edge of town.

The bank president met the sheriff in the middle of the street, took the heavily laden bags containing the "payroll" from him, and thanked him.

"Sheriff Bradford, seems to me the town's payroll's been a lot safer since you took over!"

"I'm just doing my job, Mr. Vandermeer," the sheriff said humbly. "And the job is law and order!"

The two men shook hands. The audience burst into applause, including all the members of The Saddle Club.

"That was terrific!" Lisa said. "It was so realistic, I *almost* believed it at first."

"Me, too," Carole said.

Stevie remained silent.

"Everybody does the first time they see it," Kate said.

"How did the guy roll off the porch?" Carole asked.

"There's a stack of mattresses," Kate said. "Come on, I'll show you." Lisa and Carole followed her behind the scenes of the cowboy drama.

But Stevie was distracted by the arrival of a dog. It was a big and beautiful German shepherd. The dog sniffed at Stevie's hand and then waited patiently. Stevie got the signal. She patted him on the head, and scratched behind his soft ears. His tail wagged joyfully. He sat while she patted him some more. He was wearing tags and she wanted to see if they said what his name was, but before she could read them, there was a loud whistle. The dog's ears perked up. He stood up, turned abruptly, and ran off in the direction of the whistle. Stevie completely lost him in the crowd and couldn't even see who his owner was. She shrugged to herself. It was probably somebody who would think she was just a *dude*, anyway.

She ran after her friends to see the mattresses where the "deputy" had landed. When she got there, she found that Carole and Lisa were having their pictures taken with the man who'd played the deputy. He was standing between them grinning proudly. Stevie joined in on the photograph session.

Why not? she thought, smiling to herself. After all, she *was* a dude.

5

STEWBALL GALLOPED ALONG the Pine Hollow cross-country trail. The German shepherd kept pace with the galloping horse. Stevie held a lariat in her right hand and her reins in her left. She swung the lariat up over her head where it formed a perfect circle. At just the right minute, she tossed it over the bank robber's head and yanked it tight, pinning his arms to his body. His six-shooter clattered to the ground. She waited for applause. There was none. All she heard was a whistle. The dog ran off.

Stevie sat up in bed. There was a gray darkness in the room. Her bedside clock said it was 4:45.

As she sat there, staring at the blue numbers, her very odd dream came back to her. Of course, it was just her mind piecing together the experiences she'd had in the last few days. They had been an unusual few days, to say the least. But why had she awakened?

Stevie heard the whistle again. It *hadn't* been part of her dream. It had been for real. There was something familiar about the sound, but she couldn't recall what it was or why.

Silently, Stevie crept out of bed and went to look out the porch window of the bunkhouse. It took her a few seconds to focus in the dim light of the very early morning. Her eyes identified the main house and the barn as well as silhouettes of a few trees against the horizon, where the first dim light of dawn was appearing. Then there was motion.

Stevie realized that there was another silhouette—this one of a horse and a bareback rider. She squinted her eyes. The horse stood motionless. The rider leaned forward ever so slightly, as if peering into the distance. Then there was the whistle again. It was the rider's whistle that had awakened her in the first place. Then, from behind the horse, a dog joined the horse and rider. The dog's tail wagged eagerly. The whistle was familiar; the dog looked familiar. Could it be the dog who had befriended Stevie in Two Mile Creek after the "bank robbery"?

Then, silently, the horse turned and moved off slowly. The dog trotted easily behind. Soon the threesome was completely out of Stevie's view.

She scratched her head and returned to her bunk. What kind of person would go riding at this hour of the day? What kind of person rode bareback?

"Oh," she whispered to herself. *Indians rode bareback.* Had she just seen an Indian? She sat on the bunk and then lay down and closed her eyes. Stewball broke into a canter. Stevie swung her lariat over her head in a perfect circle and tossed it at just the right moment—to lasso the Indian and his dog. . . .

"You know," Stevie said two hours later when she and her friends were sitting at the breakfast table, "I always have blueberry pancakes on my birthday. It's going to be funny eating steak and eggs this year."

"Your birthday?" Lisa said. "Is that coming up soon?"

"Yeah, it's on Saturday," Stevie told her, though she thought it was odd that Lisa didn't remember, since they'd just talked about it yesterday. "It's Alex's birthday, too," she said, turning to Kate. "He's my twin brother. Did you meet him when you were in Willow Creek?"

"No, I don't think I did," Kate said. "Pass the salt, will you?" she asked Carole. Carole handed her the saltshaker. "Eli tells me he needs some help forking hay this morning. Anybody want to pitch in?"

"I can't," Carole said. "I promised your mother I'd

show her my father's barbecue-sauce recipe right after breakfast and before we go riding."

"Me, neither," Lisa said. "I've got to get a postcard off to my mother before she starts calling every day."

"I can't, either," Kate said. "I promised lariat lessons to the Baker kids before we go on our ride. I guess Eli's stuck with the job himself." She looked meaningfully at Stevie.

If there was one thing Pine Hollow's riders learned, it was that taking care of horses was a lot of work, and they learned to help with it. Stevie couldn't believe the lame excuses her friends were coming up with to duck a fairly simple job. "*I'll* do it," she said. "I don't mind pitching hay. It's better than mucking out stalls."

"That's another advantage to keeping the horses in the pasture," Kate remarked, and they all laughed knowingly.

Stevie ate the last bite of her breakfast and cleared her dishes. If she was going to pitch hay, she might as well get to it. The sooner that was done, the sooner she and her friends could ride some more.

"See you guys," she said, and headed for the barn.

Three pairs of eyes watched her leave the mess hall.

"Mom's waiting for us in the kitchen," Kate said, pushing back from the table and grabbing her own dishes. The girls hustled, clearing quickly, and took their plates to the sink.

"Okay, now how are we going to do this?" Carole asked once the three of them and Phyllis Devine were seated at the large kitchen table. "And, most important, how are we going to keep her from knowing about it?"

"The way we'll keep her from knowing about it is easy," Phyllis said. "We just won't tell her. The bigger question is, how are we going to get that birthday cake from this kitchen to the barbecue site on Saturday without having the layers fall apart?"

"And how are we going to get her presents there without her seeing them?" Carole added.

"I've got some ideas about that," Lisa said. If we can get her out of here before breakfast for an early-morning ride, I think we can stall her until lunchtime. As long as we keep her away from the road where the pickup will be bringing all the barbecue stuff, I think it'll work. Only trouble is that it's going to mean you'll have to do all the work because *we'll* be on the trail with Stevie."

"Don't worry about that," Kate said. "You two go with her. I'll stay and help Mom. That way you can sort of get lost and she'll believe it."

Carole curled her lip in distaste. "What if we really get lost?" she asked.

"No way that could happen," Kate assured her. "The barbecue's going to be at Parson's Rock. It sticks up out of the prairie like the Empire State Building. You can find it from anywhere within miles of here."

"Sure?"

"Only a total greenhorn dude could get lost out there," Kate said. "And neither of you is that. Are you?"

Carole and Lisa exchanged glances, then giggled. There was just no telling.

"I THINK PEANUTS here needs some fresh hay," Stevie said. She was glancing into one of the barn's few box stalls where the horses needing special care were housed from time to time. "I'll get him some water, too."

"Good idea," Eli said.

There was a lot of hay and straw kept in the upper loft of the barn and it had to be pitched down as needed for food and bedding. Stevie and Eli had worked side by side until the lower bin was filled. Stevie was good at pitching hay. She knew just how to use a pitchfork. It wasn't that it was the hardest task in the world, but there were some tricks to it, and Stevie had learned them over the years at Pine Hollow. She couldn't help notice that Eli had watched her carefully, then grinned when he saw how good she was at the chore.

Stevie put the fresh hay in Peanuts's bin and filled his

bucket with cool water. While the horse took long gulps of water, she patted him comfortingly. He'd injured the tendon in his left foreleg and would be laid up for quite a while.

"It's got to be tough on him to be boxed in here after all that time outdoors, doesn't it?" she said to Eli.

He nodded. "Range horses just don't like being indoors, particularly when they're laid up like Peanuts."

"He'll get used to it, though," Stevie said. "I knew a horse once who would fuss every time he was brought into the stable—until he discovered that every time he got there, there were oats and hay waiting for him! When he'd healed and was ready to go out into the pasture, he'd just hang around the gate by the stable until somebody took pity on him and gave him a handful of oats. He was quite a horse!"

Eli looked at her quizzically. "You ride a lot?" he asked.

"Almost every day," Stevie said. "At least during the summer. In the wintertime, I usually can only ride twice a week."

"I watched you on Stewball yesterday," Eli told her.

Stevie was pretty sure he had been watching her until they'd gone around the rise behind the main house.

"You did pretty well. For a dude."

It didn't exactly *sound* like a compliment, but from Eli, Stevie suspected that it was high praise.

"I watched you cut out the riding horses yesterday," she said. "How did you train the dog?"

"I think he was born knowing how to cut horses," Eli said, taking the pitchforks and returning them to the equipment room. He took a large bucket and began mixing a blend of grains for Peanuts and the two other horses in the barn. "Wait until you see him working with cattle," Eli said.

"I've heard that dogs are really great on roundups," Stevie said. "Is it *really* instinct?"

"Some are good, some aren't," Eli told her. He poured two cans of oats into the bucket. "I've never been able to train one that wasn't."

"Have you trained a lot of them?" she asked, handing him a long-handled wooden spoon so he could mix the mash.

"Lots," he said, stirring methodically. "Lots." He seemed to be concentrating so totally on his mixture that Stevie didn't want to interrupt him for more details. When he finished blending the grains, he hung the spoon back up and stored the mixture in a cool bin. Then he put his hands on his hips and regarded Stevie carefully. She felt as if she were being x-rayed.

"Come on," he said finally. "Follow me."

He turned abruptly and left the feed room, closing the door behind him. He walked along the main aisle of the barn, past the horse stalls and the hay bins.

Almost at the end, there was an old rough wooden door, covered with cobwebs. Eli turned the handle and it swung open easily. After switching on a light, he led Stevie down some stairs into the lower-level cellar of the barn. Since the barn was built into a hill, there were only a few windows high up on one side. The floor was dirt, cool even through Stevie's boots. There was the distinct musty smell of damp earth.

Stevie followed Eli through two more doors, passing some ancient buggy tack, and even an old ox plow. Eli didn't offer any explanation of where they were going. Stevie didn't ask. She figured she'd get her answer when Eli was ready to give it.

"Quiet now," he said, but it was unnecessary. Stevie hadn't said a word since they'd left the feed room.

"Okay, girl, I'm here," he said softly, but he wasn't speaking to Stevie. Her eyes adjusted to the dim light and she heard a gentle thumping sound.

Eli crouched, sitting on his heels. Stevie crouched down next to him. There, in front of them, was a dog, her long tail thumping happily on the ground in greeting. Next to her, on top of her, all around her, climbed a whole litter of puppies, tails flailing joyously every which way.

"Oh!" Stevie said in astonishment.

"This here's Caramel," he said, introducing Stevie to the proud mother, a golden-colored dog. "I just call her Mel, though. And she's got nine pups to take care of."

"They're adorable!" Stevie said. "How old are they?" She reached out to them. Three of the puppies came over and began sniffing her curiously. Stevie patted their soft fur. One of them began licking her hand. Another nipped at her knees. The third returned to its mother, soon replaced by another who wanted to be patted, too. Stevie couldn't believe how cute they were.

"Five weeks now," Eli said. "I've been keeping them down here because Mel can be fussy sometimes and if all those dudes get wind of the pups, they'll be crawling all over the place and Mel won't like that at all."

Stevie could just imagine how difficult it would be for the mother to try and take care of her babies with a whole lot of people watching every move. She understood why Eli would want to keep this a secret. She also understood that it was a very special honor for her to learn his secret. She felt proud. She knew she had earned his trust and his respect. Maybe she wasn't just a dude anymore.

"What kind of dog is Mel?" Stevie asked, looking at her.

"Oh, I suppose she's got some shepherd in her and maybe some golden retriever. There were some huskies around here a while back. Might be she's got some of that blood. Then, that curly hair there makes me think there's some English sheepdog. I guess she's just some of everything. Everything good, that is. Mel's the best herding dog I ever had, but she's on vacation now."

"Maternity leave?" Stevie asked.

Eli looked at her and burst into laughter. "Yep," he said, nodding. "I guess that's just what you'd call it. Pups'll be ready for weaning in a week or so. Then Mel can get back to work."

"Looks to me like she's working pretty hard *now*," Stevie said. As she and Eli watched, Mel rounded up some of her rambunctious puppies, nudging a few who were using their mother as a jungle gym.

"You could be right," Eli said. "Maybe roundup will be her vacation, then. For now, though, let's leave her alone."

"Okay," Stevie said, standing up. "See you around, Mel," she said, giving the dog a final pat on her head. The dog watched as Stevie and Eli left her alone with her brood, then, just before they shut the door behind them, Mel returned her complete attention to her puppies.

"Listen, Stevie," Eli began.

"I know," she said. "It's a secret. If I promise not to

50

tell even my best friends, will you let me visit Mel again?"

"Sure thing, pardner," he said, and they shook hands to seal the deal.

Stevie found that very consoling. Maybe she was going to miss her birthday at home, but she had a secret and it was a nice one—a very nice one.

6

THE NEXT MORNING, Stevie was up again in the gray dawn, awakened by the now-familiar whistle. She swung her feet to the cool wooden floor and stood up, wondering if she could make it to the window before her mysterious Indian disappeared.

She scooted across the bunkhouse to the window, but when she couldn't see anything, she opened the door and crept out onto the porch. She stood in the shadows of the old wooden beams, watching.

There, not far from her, the Indian was riding bareback. The dog loped alongside. The horse and rider passed by the main house on the dirt road that led to the open range beyond. The Indian sat tall on the horse's back, glancing around as if to survey all the land.

An early-morning breeze ruffled Stevie's nightgown,

and the dog barked. The breeze must have carried her scent to the dog.

The rider hissed the dog into silence, pulling the horse to a stop. The Indian glanced around. Scared, without knowing why, Stevie backed farther into the shadows of the bunkhouse porch. After a few seconds, the rider urged the horse into motion and the three were soon out of sight.

Stevie remained on the porch until the odd threesome had disappeared behind a stand of cottonwood trees. She stood still long after the sound of the horse's hooves had vanished. She remained frozen in the faint gray morning light until she heard the insistent chirp of birds, announcing the advance of dawn. It startled her into motion.

She reentered the bunkhouse and climbed back into bed, but she couldn't get back to sleep. She kept wondering about the mysterious Indian who rode before dawn.

An hour later, the girls' alarm clock went off, spurring The Saddle Club into beginning the new day.

"You're not going to believe this," Stevie began, reaching for her toothbrush.

"Wha'?" Lisa asked sleepily.

"I saw an Indian," Stevie said.

"Sure, there are lots of them around," Kate said. "We see them in town all the time."

"This one wasn't in town," Stevie explained. "He

was riding along the roadway here, bareback, before the sun had come up."

"Sure you weren't dreaming?" Carole asked skeptically.

"I'm sure," Stevie stated positively, and then, as they all washed up and got ready for breakfast, she told her friends about both of the Indian's visits—and about the dog.

"I think it was the dog I saw in Two Mile Creek two days ago," Stevie said. "And I also think there's something very mysterious about this Indian riding around in the dark."

"You think he's up to something bad?" Lisa asked, a fearful tremor in her voice.

"No, it's not like that at all," Stevie assured her friend. "It's more like he's mysterious."

"Like it's an ancient ritual?" Carole asked, suddenly interested.

"Maybe," Stevie said.

"Maybe he's studying the old family burial grounds," Lisa said, following her friends' line of thought.

"Maybe it's more like he's protecting an Indian treasure buried in the mountains," Carole said, pulling on her boots.

"Maybe he's guarding the sacred hunting grounds!" Lisa suggested. Carole and Stevie looked at each other to consider the suggestion.

"And maybe you guys just need some food," Kate interrupted. "These ideas you're dreaming up are unreal! Come on, let's get going. The bell's about to—"

The triangle at the main house clanged insistently. Kate beamed with pride. "See, I told you so," she said, leading the girls to the mess hall for their morning steak and eggs.

By the time they arrived at the mess hall, three of the girls had almost forgotten Stevie's mysterious Indian. Stevie, however, could still see the proud silhouette and the spirited horse prancing in front of The Bar None.

"SO, JUST WHAT do we *do* on a roundup?" Lisa asked while the girls were finishing their breakfasts. "What's it about?"

"We do a couple of things when we round up," Kate explained. "First of all, it's when we get a chance to count our herd, find out how many calves have been born. Then, we can brand the little ones, too. Also, we can cut out the stock that is ready for sale. And, it gives us a chance to check on the herd as a whole. Sometimes you might find that there's a disease or something like that. This just gives us a chance to check them all out."

"How many cattle are there?" Lisa asked.

"We figure our land can support a herd between one

hundred twenty-five and one hundred fifty. There were a lot of calves born this spring, though. Eli thinks there may be more than one hundred fifty. We'll just see."

"What do we have to take with us?" Stevie asked. "I mean, are we going to have to carry a lot of equipment with us?"

Kate considered the question. "You know, I'm not sure," she said. "Best person to answer that is Eli. Why don't you go ask him, Stevie, while we give Mom a hand with the dishes this morning?"

"Okay," Stevie said. Dishes weren't her favorite thing and, besides, there was a piece of steak left on her plate that she thought Mel would really love. While the other girls were busy clearing, Stevie wrapped the chunk of beef into a napkin and slipped it into her pocket. Now that was a doggie bag!

"See you," she said, heading for the barn.

"Oh no you won't," Carole whispered when she knew Stevie was out of earshot. "Come on, girls, let's get back to the planning board!"

As quickly as possible, the three of them finished clearing and retreated to Phyllis's workroom, where they were creating the decorations for Stevie's party.

"You're on the banner, Lisa," Kate said. "Mom sewed a couple of bunk sheets together and we can stretch them between two trees at Parson's Rock. You can use the paint there," she said, pointing at jars of red, white, and blue paint. "It worked just fine for the barbecue we had last week."

"Okay," Lisa said, agreeable.

"Now, you can work on streamers and other decorations," Kate told Carole. "There's all kinds of crepe paper and construction paper and stuff over there."

"And what are you going to do?" Carole asked.

"I'm going into the kitchen to help my mother with the dishes so I can head Stevie off if she comes back this way. We're going to go on our trail ride in an hour and a half. Eli's taking us out to sort of prepare us for the roundup. Think you can get most of your work done before then?"

"We won't have any other time, will we?" Carole asked.

"Nope," Kate said.

"Then we'll finish," Lisa assured her.

"Sounds good to me," Kate said. She left Lisa and Carole in the workroom, closing the door behind her—just in case Stevie got nosey!

"YOU'RE GONNA NEED a clean pair of socks," Eli told Stevie. "Always got to have those."

"That's all?" she asked him.

"Well, that 'n' a lariat—nah, you won't need a lariat. Wouldn't know how to use it. Then you should have a bedroll—nah, no point in botherin' with that. Dudes like you never sleep anyway. Too worried about the rattlesnakes."

"Rattlesnakes?" Stevie said, genuine concern in her voice.

"See, I told you," Eli said. Stevie thought he could be more infuriating than anybody she had ever known in her life.

"I brought something for Mel," she said, changing the subject. She reached into her pocket and pulled out the chunk of steak. Much to Stevie's relief, Eli smiled at her. Without a word, he headed for the dark door at the back of the barn. She trailed him, eager to visit Mel and her pups again.

Mel gobbled the steak in two bites and licked Stevie's hand when she was done.

"She likes me," Stevie said.

"She likes steak," Eli said sensibly. Stevie laughed. Eli had to get back to the horses, so she couldn't visit with the puppies for very long, but she gave each one a quick pat before she and Eli returned upstairs.

Stevie went back to the main house. She found Kate in the kitchen with her mother, washing dishes. "What are Lisa and Carole doing?" she asked suspiciously.

"Peeling potatoes," Phyllis said.

Washing dishes was better than peeling potatoes any day. Stevie rolled up her sleeves to help.

"What did Eli say we should bring along?" Kate asked.

"Socks," Stevie told her. "And he said not to bother with bedrolls, since we wouldn't be able to sleep anyway."

Kate and her mother exchanged glances and burst into laughter. "He's something, isn't he?" Phyllis asked.

"Yep," Stevie agreed, trying to sound like Eli.

"Well, could you go back out there now, Stevie?" Phyllis asked. "Eli needs to tell me if he's going to want beans in the chuck-wagon chili or plain."

"Beans or plain?" Stevie asked. She hated to think how Eli was going to answer that one.

"Yep," Eli told Stevie when she asked him the question.

"Is that beans or plain?" she reiterated.

"Yep," he said.

She returned to the kitchen.

"Find out if he wants mashed or boiled potatoes," Phyllis told her once she'd gotten the answer about the chili.

Stevie shrugged, slightly annoyed, but she headed back to the barn. Eli was now busy with the family with four little children. Since it appeared that the pressing question of mashed or boiled could really wait a few hours, she didn't even try to talk to him. Instead, she went into the barn and visited with Peanuts.

The buckskin-colored horse was munching happily at his fresh hay. Stevie climbed up onto the gate that enclosed the stall and patted the horse's nose and fore-head. She told him about the dumb things she was doing that morning. Peanuts seemed to understand completely, and he didn't give her any totally dumb answers to her questions. He whinnied and nodded his head. That made her feel better.

"Ready to ride?" Carole asked, entering the barn with Lisa about a half hour later.

"Sure you're done with the potatoes?"

Stevie thought she saw a puzzled look pass between Lisa and Carole.

"Of course they are," Kate said, coming up behind them. "All the chores are done. Time for a trail ride and a lesson on roundups."

Eli helped the girls get their horses out of the corral. By then, each girl could manage her own tack, even with Eli's suspicious gaze watching every motion, so they were saddled-up and ready to ride in just a few minutes.

Eli was on his horse, too. The five of them left the corral and, instead of taking the trail the girls had ridden before, they headed for the open range—the same direction Stevie's mysterious Indian had taken.

Eli didn't say much as they rode, but what he did say turned out to be worth listening too. He told them that their first concern had to be the calves. "Where there's a calf, there's a cow," he said. "Watch out for her if she thinks you're going to hurt her young 'un. And sometimes a big old bull will get an idea that he ought to be in charge of the roundup. If that happens, you get out of the way. He's bigger than you. Probably smarter, too. Me and the dog will show him the way."

He explained that they'd begin by riding to the far end of the property, where the herd had been seen grazing the week before, and they'd drive them all back to the ranch.

"We'll see some strays on the way out, but we'll pick them up on our way back. They're easier to herd if we've got a hundred and fifty head with us to convince them along."

He told them what to expect if the cattle got frightened and he explained how they'd stay nearby while they camped. Stevie was glad to see that with Kate there, he didn't make a lot of smart remarks about rattlesnakes and dudes.

"Most of the time," he told the girls, "we'll be riding along like this." It was a pleasant pace. The horses walked smoothly across the open land, giving the girls the time to admire the landscape with its snow-topped mountains as a breathtaking backdrop. "And sometimes, it's like this," Eli said.

In an instant, Eli's horse began to gallop, as if he were chasing a stray. He rode up an incline and along the top of a ridge, leaving a cloud of dust behind him. When he reached the top of the ridge, Eli turned the horse to his left and disappeared on the other side without slowing his pace one bit.

Kate looked over her shoulder at her friends. They all knew they'd been challenged. And they accepted.

Kate gave her horse a kick and he sprang into action. Kate and Spot nearly flew up the hillside. Lisa on Chocolate and Carole on Berry followed close behind. Stevie pressed her calves on Stewball's sides, but the horse stood still.

Suddenly, she got the feeling that her first instinct about this funny-looking horse had been right. He was going to be stubborn and unpredictable and Eli had chosen him for her just to be a tease. But then Stewball proved her wrong.

While Berry and Chocolate struggled up the steep side of the hill, Stewball turned in the opposite direction and reached the top by a gentler slope. The only problem was that it wasn't at all what Stevie had told him to do! With little or no help from Stevie, Stewball led the way. The horse clearly understood the challenge, too, and was determined to meet it head-on. Stevie remembered that horses are extremely competitive animals.

Ahead, through the dust, she could see Eli, still galloping fiercely. Stevie leaned forward toward Stewball's brown-and-white mane. "Get 'im, Stewball," she said. Those seemed to be the words the horse wanted to hear.

Stevie held on as he spurted ahead, gripping tightly with her legs, holding the reins loosely enough to give Stewball the slack he needed. She settled into the saddle and let her horse do the work.

Stewball's pace quickened and his stride lengthened. Berry and Chocolate were well behind and the gap between Stewball and Eli was narrowing. Stevie could see that the end of the race was near. Ahead, perhaps a hundred yards, a creek cut across the land. It was a welcome sight. They'd all need some refreshment by the time they got there.

Stewball began going even faster. Stevie could feel the dust kicked up by Eli's horse in her eyes, taste it in her mouth. If it bothered Stewball, there was no way of telling. It just seemed to make him go faster. Stevie had never felt anything like the controlled energy beneath her now.

"Go for it, Stewball!" she said excitedly. The horse's ears flicked back as if he understood her words, then flattened in determination.

The creek was only a few yards ahead now and Stevie could almost touch Eli's horse. She leaned forward, watching as her horse's nose passed by Eli's horse. She'd won!

Grinning, and breathing hard with excitement, she sat upright in the saddle and pulled gently on the reins. Stewball was ready to stop. Smoothly, he slowed his pace until he was walking. He held his head high.

"That what you wanted to show us how to do?" Stevie asked Eli.

He regarded her carefully. "Something like that," he agreed.

"Well, to tell you the truth, I don't know about me, but I'm pretty sure Stewball can handle it."

"I'm pretty sure he can," Eli agreed, grinning in spite of himself.

The two dismounted and waited for Lisa, Carole, and Kate to catch up to them.

"I never saw anything like it!" Kate said, sliding down off Spot. "Stewball's amazing!"

"Yep," Eli said.

"Are you sure he's coming back?" Carole asked Stevie the next morning. The four girls were in their bathrobes, standing barefoot on the porch of their bunkhouse. It was still dark, the first hints of dawn on the eastern horizon.

"Of course not," Stevie said. "But you don't want to miss it if he does, do you? After all, there may be an Indian treasure, or maybe we'll learn some kind of ritual thing. I read once where some Indians, when they get to be about our age, spend weeks at a time in the wilderness. Maybe that's what this guy's doing."

"I read that book, too," Lisa said. "It took place more than a hundred years ago—and it was fiction."

"Well, maybe, but how about the idea of treasure?

You know, something hidden from marauding settlers for centuries."

"I like *that* one," Lisa said. "But I don't believe it."

"Neither do I," Stevie admitted. Then, while her mind raced through other exciting possibilities, she heard the hoofbeats she'd been waiting for. "There," she said. "He's coming."

All four girls filed down off the porch and began making their way toward the roadway with the help of the dim light of the gray dawn.

Although the girls tried to stay in the shadows, they weren't hidden to the dog. He began barking excitedly. He romped over to the foursome and began wagging his tail joyously while he sniffed at Stevie. She knew then for sure that it was the same dog she'd met in town the day of the "bank robbery." They patted him and watched his tail swish.

"Who's there?" the rider asked.

"I'm Kate Devine," Kate said, stepping out of the shadows. "I live here with my parents. This is our ranch. Who are you?"

"I'm Christine Lonetree," the rider said, sitting easily on the bare back of her horse. "This is my dog, Tomahawk, and my horse, Arrow."

Christine??? Stevie said to herself. It wasn't an Indian boy at all. It was an Indian girl and she was about their age!

66

"Are you an *Indian?*" Lisa asked. The awe was clear in her voice.

"Sure," Christine answered, laughing gently. "You a paleface?" She dismounted and held Arrow's rein loosely.

"Oh," Lisa said, embarrassed. "I didn't mean it that way. . . ."

"I know," Christine said. "People never do. Say, what are you doing up at this hour? I thought all dudes were asleep at least until lunchtime."

"Actually, we were waiting for you," Stevie confessed. "I saw you yesterday morning and the day before. I was curious."

"So that's why Tomahawk barked," Christine said. "I was wondering."

"He knew me already," Stevie explained. "We met in town the other day. He was at the bank robbery. Were you there, too?"

"Watching the McClanahan gang try to steal the payroll?" Christine said, laughing. "No, I was just running an errand at the jewelry store. Tomahawk got lost in the crowd."

"Does he always come when you whistle?" Stevie asked.

"Always," Christine said.

"How come you go out for a ride so early in the morning?" Stevie asked.

"I like it. You have a problem with it?" she challenged.

"No, you can ride whenever you want," Stevie said quickly. "We just wondered if there was some special reason why it had to be so early."

"Yeah, like if it's some sort of ritual," Lisa added.

"You know, to protect the spirits of your ancestors," Carole said.

"Or the treasure hidden from the marauding settlers," Stevie said.

"Give me a break," Christine said. "I ride at this hour because I *like* to ride at this hour. So does my horse. And it's cooler at this time of day—in case you *dudes* hadn't noticed it."

"You don't have to get so upset," Stevie said. "We were just wondering."

"Well, wonder about somebody else," Christine said. "I'm not some kind of freak who does rain dances in the moonlight or sprinkles mustard seeds on sacred hunting grounds."

She remounted her horse and turned to leave the girls.

Stevie had a sick feeling in the pit of her stomach. She realized that their dumb guesses about Christine's dawn riding had really hurt the girl's feelings, and she hadn't meant to do that at all.

"Hey, I'm sorry," Stevie said. "We didn't mean to hurt your feelings. We were just curious—"

"Well, go be curious about whether the clothes you're wearing are fancy enough or if your hat is eight or ten gallons or whether you can talk the wrangler into taking care of your horse for you!"

With that, Christine turned Arrow back the way she had come. The horse picked up a trot and then a lope. As she rode away, the long, familiar whistle trailed behind her.

Tomahawk, who had been sitting at Stevie's feet, stood up and ran after Christine.

The girls remained still and watched while the young Indian girl, her horse, and her dog crossed the open land toward the darker horizon to the west, returning home.

"What a funny girl," Lisa remarked. "I guess we hurt her feelings."

"And I guess she hurt ours," Stevie grumbled. "She sure has a lot of dumb ideas about dudes."

"And I guess we had a lot of dumb ideas about Indians," Carole reminded her.

"I guess the dumbest idea was getting up at that hour to meet him—I mean her," Stevie said.

"No," Carole said pensively. "I think it was worth it. I just wish it had gone differently."

The girls turned and retreated to their bunkhouse. The sun had reached the eastern mountaintops and the sky was brightening. In the darkness of the west, a few pale stars were still visible as a reminder of the night gone by. In the east, the streaks of daylight reminded the girls of the challenge of the day that lay before them.

"Hey, we're going on a roundup today!" Stevie howled with excitement.

"Yippie ki yi yay!" Lisa exclaimed.

"*Don't* let Eli hear you saying that!" Stevie said.

"Only dumb dudes say it, huh?" Lisa said.

Kate nodded, trying to look serious. "The kind that wear eight-gallon hats and get wranglers to take care of their horses for them."

"Okay, then, how about tallyho?" Lisa suggested.

"*Much* better," Kate said, giggling.

The girls decided to set aside their uncomfortable memories of their meeting with Christine Lonetree and concentrate on the fun they just knew they were going to have on the long-awaited roundup.

8

It took the riders more than half a day to reach the most distant point of their ride. The group was comprised of nine people. There were two wranglers, Eli and Jeff. Then there were the four girls, one of the older couples who were staying at the ranch, and Frank Devine. Stevie suspected that Eli and Jeff could probably manage the roundup all by themselves, but she was still glad to be along. After all, there was an awful lot to learn.

As Eli had predicted, they'd seen a number of strays on their way out. The strays were grazing in the green pastures near the creeks or hanging out under the shade trees. The girls had even spotted a very young calf with its mother. It was cute as could be, with long knobby-kneed legs.

"Kind of reminds me of Samson," Carole remarked.

"All baby animals remind you of Samson," Stevie teased. "But then, all baby animals are cute, just like Samson is."

"Did you ever see a baby rhinoceros?" Lisa asked. The girls told her they hadn't. "Only a mother could love it," she told her friends. "It wouldn't remind you of Samson at all."

"All right, but that calf there *did* remind me of Samson," Carole said.

"Hey, the dog seems excited," Stevie observed. Eli's dog began circling playfully, alertly. It was as if it could tell that the fun was about to begin. "What's over the hill?"

"I have this picture of spotting the pretty rust-and-white markings on the animals as they graze," Carole remarked.

"And *I* thought we'd hear the gentle lowing," Lisa added.

"You'll hear the lowing when we start driving them," Kate said. "But there's nothing gentle about it. These animals make a real racket! The cows moo to call to their calves. They don't want to be separated."

Eli and Jeff were leading the riders. Their horses picked up speed as they approached the herd, sniffing the dusty air as if anticipating the familiar smell of cattle.

The Saddle Club members all sped up their horses as well. Stevie thought she could feel Stewball's excitement. His breath quickened. His stride lengthened. His ears perked straight up and then twitched alertly.

The horses carried their riders to the crest of a gentle hill. Stevie was expecting to spot their quarry as soon as they reached the top, but it was farther than she thought. The cattle were beyond the *next* hill. But they were there. She could feel her own heart beat a little faster with the excitement.

Sometimes, in old cowboy movies, she'd seen eager cowboys come galloping up to a herd of cattle to get them moving, but Eli had made it clear that nobody, *but nobody*, was to gallop up to the herd. What could happen was about the most dangerous thing there was. If the cattle were startled by a galloping horse, they could stampede. A stampede might seem like a neat piece of action on a movie screen, but in real life it could be very dangerous. The frightened cattle would run any way they could, without thinking about it at all. Stampeding cattle ran over each other; they ran into horses; they could even run off cliffs.

Eli's horse slowed to a very gentle walk as they rounded the next hill.

There, in a little valley formed by small hills and fed by a fresh stream, more than a hundred head of cattle were grazing contentedly. A few of them lifted their heads from the grass to eye the riders, but they quickly returned their attention to the grass in front of them.

"Oh, look!" Lisa said. The girls gazed where she pointed. There, at the edge of the herd, was a small group, grazing a little distance apart from the others. There were about seven very young calves, and their mothers.

"I guess that's the day-care center," Carole quipped.

As Eli had instructed them, all of the riders circled to the far side of the herd. Then, at Eli's signal, they began walking slowly and easily, interrupting the lazy grazing of the cattle. As the riders passed the cattle, they lifted their heads from the grass and began walking away from the horses. As soon as a few started moving, the rest quickly joined them, first walking very slowly, and then picking up their pace. As Kate had predicted, the loud mooing began almost immediately.

Eli wanted the herd to return the same way the riders had come. He and Jeff moved back and forth on horseback, almost effortlessly, keeping the cattle going in the right direction. In contrast to the easy pace of the horses, Eli's dog moved quickly, dodging to the left and to the right, growling occasionally at a steer who might, for a moment, think he ought to head in some other direction.

Kate's father had circled to the near side of the pack, leading the herd. "Once a steer decides he wants to follow something, almost nothing will make him change his mind," Eli had told the girls earlier. "The trick is to get him to want to follow a horse."

The cattle were following Frank docilely.

The herd began moving a little more quickly once the leaders had rounded the first hill and they could see open land in front of them. The girls' horses automatically kept pace with the cattle. Stevie, knowing that Stewball could outrun any steer in the herd (and any other horse, as well), wasn't concerned about being left behind. But she was still relieved that the herd seemed to have reached a steady pace.

"This is *fun*," Lisa remarked, pulling up next to her. "Don't you think so?"

"I sure do," Stevie agreed. "I've never done anything like this. Can you believe the horses and the dog?"

"Incredible!" Carole exclaimed. "We're used to horses you have to control at every move. Even though you still have to control these horses as far as riding is concerned, when it comes to herding, I'm beginning to get the feeling they could do this without us."

"Hey! Dudes!" It was Eli, calling the girls. "Watch out for that little 'un over there!" He was pointing to their left. They looked to see a small calf, limping along. Its mother was nudging the baby from behind, but the calf appeared to have injured his leg, making it difficult for him to keep up with the rest of the herd.

Lisa stayed with the herd. Carole and Stevie turned their horses around and went back to see if anything could be done for the calf. Carole got down from her horse, handing Stevie the reins. The cow eyed her dubiously. Carole gave the mother a reassuring pat on the head. Stevie brought Stewball between the cow and Carole, in case she changed her mind about Carole, but she didn't think Carole was in danger.

Stevie admired that about Carole. Put her on her feet in the middle of a herd of one hundred fifty cattle, and she'll still find a way to make friends with a worried cow, Stevie thought as Carole stroked the calf's shoulders reassuringly.

"What's the problem?" Stevie asked.

"He's gotten himself all tangled in strands of dry grass. It's like he's hobbled," she said. "Did you bring a knife with you?"

"The only thing Eli told me to bring was a pair of clean socks," Stevie said. "But I didn't listen to him. Sure I've got my pocketknife." She fished deep into her jeans and pulled out her old Girl Scout knife. "It's sharp, too, you'll be glad to know."

She watched as Carole expertly freed the calf from the mass of twigs and grass that had entrapped him. He fussed a bit as she worked, and then tried to nibble at her shoulder.

"Give me a break, will you?" Carole joked to the brown-and-white calf.

The cow tired of waiting. She began to nudge harshly at Stevie and Stewball. Stevie shifted uneasily in the saddle, uncertain what to do. The cow seemed to sense her fear and increased her attack, but stopped abruptly at the sharp report of a dog's bark. The cow backed off. Stevie looked for Eli's dog, but she saw instead the bushy coat of a German shepherd disappearing in the dust of the herd. It looked like Tomahawk, but that didn't seem likely. She shrugged the thought off and turned her attention to Carole's project, which was almost done.

In another few seconds the job was finished. Carole stood back and watched the cow and her calf. The mother eyed him curiously as he took one tentative step, then another. When she could see the calf was free, the cow nudged him forward again and they were soon trotting along with the rest of the herd.

Carole remounted Berry, who had stood by placidly.

"Where's the little 'un?" Eli asked, riding up to them as they were ready to proceed.

"Right over there," Carole said. "He'd just gotten tangled in some grass. I cut it off his hooves. He's fine now."

Eli regarded her curiously. "Didn't the cow give you some trouble?"

"She didn't trust me at first, but we got along okay in the end."

"I guess you did," Eli said. With that, he urged his horse into a trot and got back to the work of herding.

"I think you just got an A-plus in roundups," Stevie said.

"I think you're right. I was expecting him to say, 'Not bad—for a *dude.*'" Stevie giggled.

"What's so funny?" Lisa asked, riding up to join them.

"Oh, it's just Eli," Stevie told her. "Carole just practically saved the life of a calf, risking her own at the same time, and Eli just gives her a nod."

"Way to go!" Lisa said. "You must have been something to get a whole nod from Eli."

Carole wanted to change the subject. "Come on," she said. "We're going to cross the creek a couple of hundred yards ahead. That should be interesting."

The three girls and their horses hurried to catch up with the others, keeping a sharp eye out for strays as they went.

Stevie could see the creek when they rounded the next hillside. Eli had warned them that some of the calves could have trouble with the water, but this was a shallow crossing. She didn't think any of the animals would have a problem with the rocks and water.

Like the other riders, Stevie had gotten used to the constant noise of the cattle. It sounded a bit like a traffic jam at rush hour. The moos were like honking horns, all indistinguishable from one another, all just part of the general herd noise.

But then she heard another honking, this one louder, more insistent, somehow more serious. Stevie looked over her shoulder to where she thought the sound came from. At first, all she saw was a dry patch of brush. Then she saw it wiggle. She turned Stewball around to get a better look. Soon she realized that some of what she thought was just brown bush was actually brown calf. There was a frightened bleating sound as the calf bellowed for attention once again. He was in trouble and he was scared.

Stevie and Stewball rode over to the calf. Before she dismounted, she wanted to have a plan so that she wouldn't frighten the calf before she could be sure she could help him. She realized that the brown bush was a thorny bush, and that the thorns seemed to have caught in the calf's soft hair. It was going to take a lot of work to get him loose. She thought she'd better get started right away.

Stevie spotted a place where she could hitch Stewball while she worked. It wouldn't do to have him wander off. Carole and Lisa were farther ahead, and Kate was riding with her father. Stevie swung her right leg over the saddle and was about to lower herself to the ground when she heard a sound she couldn't confuse with anything else in the whole wide world.

It was the sound of a rattlesnake, shaking his rattle furiously, about to strike!

Stewball knew the sound, too, and it scared him. He reared in terror, tossing Stevie to the ground like a sack of potatoes, then galloped off as fast as his legs could carry him.

At that instant, the little calf broke loose all by himself and trotted off to find his mother.

Stevie landed in the dusty earth by the thornbush. She landed hard on her side and hit her head on the ground. She was dizzy, and sore, and confused. For a moment, the world was a haze in which there was the distant bellowing of an unhappy calf, the vague pain in her ribs, and the sound of a horse's hoofbeats, retreating. But one thing was clear. The rattling hadn't stopped. When Stevie turned her head, she saw it.

There, not two feet from her, coiled to strike, was a diamondback rattler.

And his target was Stevie!

9

THE ONLY SOUND Stevie could hear was the viper's rattling. The mooing of the herd and the thump of their hooves on the dry ground faded to a distant sound, insignificant compared to the insistent danger warning of the snake.

Then she heard a dog bark. Stevie's eyes were riveted on the snake's, and his to hers. She couldn't see a dog, she was only barely aware of its presence. The dog growled.

The snake rose up, as if to see better. Every instinct Stevie had told her to flee, but she had the feeling that this snake liked moving targets. She was frozen where she sat in the dust, just a few feet away from the deadly creature.

The dog barked again. This time it was very close.

Stevie could hear him panting excitedly as he approached her and the snake. She didn't even dare to turn and see what kind of dog it was, but there was something familiar about the bark. And then, there was something even more familiar about the whistle that followed it.

Tomahawk barked again and then growled at the snake. The dog crept between Stevie and the snake and bared his teeth at the rattler.

Stevie looked up and behind her. Christine Lonetree was there, on her horse.

"It's a rattler," Stevie said. "Please help me!"

"You're going to have to help yourself," Christine said. "Back up slowly. Get out of the snake's range. And get out of Tomahawk's way."

Stevie inched backward slowly but steadily, keeping her eye on the dog who stood between her and the rattlesnake. When she could, she stood up and retreated, still watching the two animals face off.

When she was about fifteen feet away, she circled the scene, standing near to where Christine was holding her horse still. Even the horse could sense danger. His nostrils flared and his ears lay back almost flat on his head.

When Christine was sure Stevie was safe, she whistled for Tomahawk. The dog's ears flicked at the sound, but his body didn't move and his eyes never left the snake.

Christine and Stevie watched in horror.

Tomahawk took a step forward, sniffing. The snake backed up. Its tongue flicked out. When it moved forward again, Tomahawk withdrew. The snake held still. Tomahawk advanced again. The snake remained where it was. Tomahawk growled. The snake snapped backward. Tomahawk bared his teeth. The snake shifted forward again. Tomahawk barked. The snake stood still for a second, then shifted backward.

It was like a primitive dance, acted out between ancient enemies. Neither seemed to want to strike. Neither seemed to want to back down.

The snake shook its rattle harder. That distracted Tomahawk. He glanced at the creature's tail and reached forward with his nose. But this time he'd gone too far.

In an instant, the rattlesnake shot forward and punctured the dog's shiny black nose with his deadly fangs. Later Stevie wondered if she'd actually seen it happen, or if it had been too fast for the human eye.

Tomahawk yowled, first in surprise, then in pain. He shook his head violently while the snake hung on, injecting his deadly poison into Christine's German shepherd.

"Oh, no!" Stevie screamed. "It can't be!" She wanted to run to the dog to help him. She wanted to kill the murderous snake with her bare hands. She wanted revenge.

"Don't move!" Christine commanded.

Stevie froze.

It was over in a few seconds. The snake removed itself from Tomahawk, sank to the ground, and slithered off into the underbrush. Tomahawk, already weak from the poison, stumbled over to his mistress. Stevie was closer to the dog and caught him before he fell. She sat down and held the dog's head in her lap.

"You saved my life, boy!" Stevie said to Tomahawk, patting him gently on his shoulder. Tears came to her eyes. "The snake got you, not me. You saved my life!"

The dog panted, breathing irregularly. He looked up into Stevie's eyes and blinked. It almost seemed as if he were trying to reassure her, to tell her it was right that he should die and she should live. Then he shuddered.

Stevie cradled him gently, patting him, talking to him. Christine knelt next to them, frozen in shock, listening blankly to Stevie's comforting words to Tomahawk. Stevie didn't know what she was saying, but she wanted the dog to know that he was with someone who knew what he'd done, how he'd chosen to die in her place, and how thankful she was.

84

His tongue came out once to lick her hand. And then his eyes closed forever.

There was a silence then, more profound than any Stevie had ever known in her life. She held the dog as his life left him. Tears streamed down her face.

"He's dead," she told Christine when she looked up. "Tomahawk died saving me. He was a wonderful dog, and now he's dead," she finished desolately.

Christine's face was filled with the same deep sadness that Stevie felt. Christine didn't even *like* Stevie, but her dog had given up his life for hers.

"I'm sorry," Stevie said. It wasn't nearly enough, but it was the only thing she could say.

Slowly, Stevie stood up. She lifted Tomahawk's limp body, still warm with the life he'd lived so joyously. She carried the dog solemnly over to where Christine had hitched Arrow. "You'll want to bury him, won't you?" Stevie asked.

Christine nodded.

Together, Stevie and Christine lifted the dog's body carefully and placed him across the horse's back.

"One of the wranglers will have a shovel," Stevie told Christine. "I bet Tomahawk would like to rest on the shore of that creek over there. There's a nice green patch at the base of the hill."

Christine was silent.

10

"Hey, Stevie, are you all right?"

It was Carole. Stevie turned around from Christine's horse to see her leading Stewball.

"Stewball came running around the hill like he'd gone crazy—and when we didn't see you . . . Well, I'm glad to see you're okay. Did he throw you? Did you get hurt? Shall we get the first-aid kit from Eli?"

"I'm all—"

"Oh, *there* you are, Stevie," Lisa said, arriving breathlessly on Chocolate. "I'm so relieved that everything's all right! You can't imagine what we . . ." She looked at Stevie's face and knew immediately that everything was *not* all right.

"What *happened?*" Carole asked, deeply concerned.

Just then, Kate pulled up on her horse. "Hello,

Christine," she said politely, acknowledging the girl's presence. Then she, too, asked what had happened.

Stevie had been standing in front of Arrow. Until she stepped aside, none of the girls could see Tomahawk's lifeless body across the horse's back.

"Oh, no!" Carole said, looking stricken at the sight. "Is he . . . ?"

Christine nodded. "It was a rattlesnake," she said. Then she paused to compose herself. "She was on the ground," she said, pointing to Stevie, "and the snake was about to strike, and . . ." She had trouble going on.

"What she means is that Tomahawk saved my life," Stevie said simply. Then she described the terrible events that led to the snake's attack on the dog.

Christine took over. "And she held my dog," she told the girls. "She held him through his painful last minutes, and let him know he wasn't alone."

"It was the least I could do," Stevie said, surprised that Christine was apparently touched by her own kindness to Tomahawk. "Now, I'd like to help you bury him. Do you girls want to help, too, or do you have to keep up with the herd?"

"The herd'll do just fine without us for a while," Kate assured Stevie. "In fact, I get the impression from Eli sometimes that the roundup actually goes *better* without the dudes along."

87

Stevie smiled slightly. That was just like Eli. But she wouldn't be surprised if it was true. "Yep, he thinks we're just dumb dudes," she said.

Christine looked at Stevie thoughtfully for a moment. "I think I've been guilty of that, too," she said. There was an awkward silence.

"I'll go get the shovel from Eli," Kate offered after a moment. "I'll tell him we'll be with them at the lunch stop. I'll meet you guys down by the creek."

Kate turned Spot around to catch up with the herd. The other girls dismounted and walked their horses across the range to the creek.

As they walked, they introduced themselves to Christine, since they'd never even had a chance to tell her their names. Stevie was very aware of the sad task ahead of them, but she couldn't help feeling that Tomahawk's death was signaling a birth of friendship between The Saddle Club and Christine Lonetree. Certainly, the girls were coming to understand one another as they never could have done before.

"Say, where did you girls learn to ride?" Christine asked. Stevie and her friends understood that Christine was trying to keep from showing her emotions by changing the subject. They followed her lead.

Lisa explained that they were friends because they all studied riding at Pine Hollow Stables in Willow Creek, Virginia.

"English?" Christine asked.

"Of course," Carole said. "But you know, horses are horses. And while there are differences in riding styles, there are a lot more similarities."

"I think I'm learning that it's the same with people," Christine said, drawing to a stop at the bank of the creek.

"The main problem seems to be when people start thinking things about other people when they don't have the facts," Stevie added.

"You mean like the Western idea that 'dumb dude' is really one word?"

"Or the idea that an Indian riding in the early dawn must be on some ancient tribal mission."

"Oh, yeah, like protecting the treasure from the marauding settlers," Christine said, smiling at last. "To tell you the truth, I really liked that one!" She began laughing and the girls were only too pleased to laugh with her—at themselves.

Kate arrived then with the shovel. Their thoughts returned to their sad mission. They took turns digging a grave in the cool earth. It didn't take long and as they worked, the girls found consolation in the idea that Tomahawk's resting place *was* a beautiful one.

When the grave was finished, Christine and Stevie placed the dog in it. Then they looked awkwardly at each other, wondering if they should say a prayer. Stevie answered the question for them. She spoke to the dog.

"Tomahawk," she began. "We're going to leave you here in this beautiful place. If you can hear us, wherever you are now, you'll know that Christine thanks you for your wonderful life, and I thank you for saving me with your death. If there's a god of dogs, he'll take care of you. Amen."

The girls echoed Stevie's "Amen," and then quickly filled in the grave. When they were done, only a soft mound of earth marked Tomahawk's resting place. But where he lay in death didn't seem to matter anywhere near as much as what he had done in life.

Solemnly, the girls turned and led their horses away from Tomahawk's grave.

"Time to catch up with the wranglers," Kate said. "They'll be moving along any minute now." She turned to their new friend. "Christine," she said, "we'll be back at The Bar None tomorrow. Would you like to come over to visit?"

Christine smiled. "I've got a better idea," she said. "I'll answer your questions about my morning ride. I'll come for you at four-thirty the next morning. Be ready to ride. Bareback."

With that, Christine turned to Arrow and boosted herself up onto his back. Taking his reins in one hand, she turned from her new friends and the horse took off at a lope.

The Saddle Club turned to their own horses. It was time to get on with the roundup.

"Git along little dogie!" Lisa began to sing, off-key.

"I think I like the one about 'Yippie ki yi yay' better," Stevie remarked as they began their return to the herd.

"I think I like it better when you can't hear her over the moos of the cattle," Carole said.

The girls laughed together.

THE GIRLS WERE very busy for the rest of the roundup. Before they got to the next creek crossing, they had to cover a vast open section of the range. The herd began to spread out and wander. Also, since there had been a number of strays remaining in this section, the herd tended to wander toward the strays, instead of the other way around.

Eli directed all the riders to surround the herd while he and Jeff rounded up strays, bringing them into the main herd. But while they were waiting, the herd seemed to sense the nearness of the creek ahead and there was no containing it. The cattle headed straight for the water and then spread out along the banks of the creek so they could all get drinks.

The girls circled back and forth along the edge of

the herd just as they'd seen Eli and Jeff doing. It was very different riding from anything they'd ever done before. Not only did they have to be careful what they were doing as riders, controlling their horses, but they also had to keep eagle eyes on the herd as it meandered this way and that.

Stevie was breathing hard with fatigue and excitement as she and Stewball trotted after a cow and her calf who were wandering downstream. Stewball seemed to know what to do with very little prompting from Stevie. She let him take charge—and when the cow decided to dodge him, Stewball *really* took charge. He leapt to the left, blocking the cow's escape. The cow stopped short, and gave Stewball a look. Stevie couldn't see Stewball's face, but from the way the cow then sheepishly returned to the herd, she figured it must have been something!

"Good boy," she said, patting him affectionately on the neck.

Finally, the herd was assembled at the edge of the creek and they began the crossing. The girls were assigned spots in the middle of the creek and on either side of the herd, to see that none of the cattle would stray in the middle of the crossing. The horses stood contentedly in the water. The girls suspected the cool creek felt good on the animals' hot feet.

Stevie watched while the herd sloshed across the

creek. It had rained the week before so the water level was quite high and the stream was flowing rapidly. Most of the cattle didn't even seem to notice the water at all, except to take a sip at the bank. But there was one calf who was having trouble. Its mother watched it with apparent concern.

He was almost all a reddish-brown color with a bright pink nose and little eyes that sparkled in the daylight. He was much smaller than most of the other calves in the herd and it seemed that the majority of him was spindly legs with knobby knees—and those spindly legs were having quite a time with the rushing water. At first, he was okay, but when he got a few steps out into the creek, it was clear that he was having trouble holding his balance. He stepped sideways, downstream, his legs being pushed by the water. Stevie realized that if he took one more step forward, the rush of the water was going to be too much for him, and he might drown.

She'd already watched one animal die that day, and she wasn't going to see it happen again.

Stevie turned to Carole. "Come on. We've got a job to do." The two of them went over to where the little calf was quaking in the water. The creek was about a foot deep there—not deep enough to cause Stevie and Carole harm, but just deep enough to get their boots soaking wet. Stevie consoled herself with the knowledge that she did, after all, have a clean pair of socks with her.

The girls slid down off their horses and, wrapping the reins around their wrists, they leaned over to pick up the little calf together. It was still struggling against the water. He may have been a little calf, but he was heavy. Using every ounce of their strength, and working in perfect unity, they lifted the calf up to Stewball's withers.

"Let me get on the other side to make sure he's not just going to slide off," Carole said. She dodged under Stewball's neck, taking hold of the calf's front hooves. "Push him a bit!" Carole told Stevie.

Stevie hefted the calf, evading the angry kicking of his rear hooves. "I don't think he likes this much," she told Carole. "I don't think I'd like it much either," she added.

"Beats drowning," Carole reminded her.

The girls shifted the calf's weight a couple of times. When they were pretty sure he was balanced, Carole remounted Berry and held Stewball's reins for Stevie, keeping the horse steady under his new and heavy burden. Stevie rose in the stirrups carefully, sitting right behind the straddled calf. Carole handed her Stewball's reins. "Good luck!" she said.

Stevie had the feeling she was going to need it. She adjusted the calf against her thighs so he wouldn't slide off, and proceeded across the creek. The calf protested his rather uncomfortable position with grunts and bleats. Stevie tried to pat him, but that just made him kick and *that* could lead to disaster. She started to sing to him. "Git along, little dogie, git along!" He calmed down. Stevie figured that meant he liked her singing; or maybe it just sounded like the cows' moos! Whatever the reason, it worked. The calf lay quietly, and its mother followed Stewball obediently.

When she and Carole reached the far side of the creek, Eli spotted them, and grinned broadly at Stevie.

"I'll make a wrangler of you yet," he said. "Never did that on one of your sissy English trail rides, did you?"

Stevie knew it was a compliment, so she smiled back at him. "I'm learning," she said. "But how do I get this guy down from here?"

Eli rode over to her. He dismounted and helped Stevie remove the calf from Stewball's withers. Stewball stood absolutely still even when the calf's sharp hooves scraped across his withers. Stevie was admiring the horse more and more with every passing minute.

"Here you go, boy," Eli said, slapping the rump of the startled calf. "Time to go to Mama!"

The cow approached her newborn, sniffed him a few times, glanced at Stewball and Stevie, then nudged the calf ahead. In a few seconds, the pair had merged with the herd and it was soon impossible for Stevie to tell just which calf it was that she had saved from drowning.

THAT NIGHT, STEVIE lay in her bedroll, staring up at the million stars that were sprinkled across the sky like so many grains of spilled sugar on black velvet. She thought with sadness about Tomahawk's death, and then she remembered Eli's dog, Mel, and her puppies. Stevie wondered whether one of Mel's puppies could ever make up for Tomahawk, but she knew that an animal like that *couldn't* be replaced. She hoped she'd be able to think of some way to thank Christine, but she knew it wasn't by trying to fill Tomahawk's place.

She thought about the other things that had happened during the day. She couldn't remember a more eventful day in her whole life, or a day in which she'd had more new experiences. It had been an odd mix of fear, sadness, friendship, happiness, love. Eli was right that there was a lot to learn. But despite her hectic, even traumatic, day, Stevie fell into a deep, dreamless sleep almost immediately.

WHEN MORNING CAME, there was just a short ride before the herd arrived at the ranch. The riders brought the herd into the corrals at The Bar None before lunchtime. The girls watched while the wranglers cut and counted the herd and while the calves were branded with The Bar None symbol. Stevie thought she could tell which calf she'd carried across the creek, but when she saw another almost like it, she wasn't so sure.

"Come on, let's go shower and change our clothes before lunch," Kate suggested to her friends.

"Why?" Stevie asked. "We'll just ride again after lunch, won't we?"

"Probably," Kate agreed. "But would you really want to sit next to yourself at lunch after two days on the trail?"

The girls laughed. They *did* smell like horses, and cattle, and dust.

"I guess a shower isn't such a bad idea after all," Stevie agreed. "And, of course, a change of socks!"

"I CAN'T BELIEVE how hungry I am!" Lisa said, looking at her plate. "Why, I must have had two helpings of everything!"

"You had *three* helpings of rolls," Carole teased. "But don't worry, I did, too. Everything out here tastes so good."

"That's because you can really build up an appetite herding cattle," Kate said. "I told you so, didn't I?"

"I think I'll give herding a rest for a few days," Stevie said, "but I'm ready to go for another ride. When shall we go out?" she asked.

Kate, Lisa, and Carole exchanged looks. Stevie wondered what *that* was about.

"I think I've done enough riding for the day," Lisa said. "I wanted to take some time to send my mother another postcard, maybe take a nap this afternoon. I didn't sleep all that well last night."

"Me, too," Kate said. "Besides, my mom asked me to give her a hand with a chore."

"Carole?" Stevie asked.

"I promised the little kids I'd show them how to tack up a horse. They want to use the ponies and Eli's too busy with the cutting and branding."

Stevie couldn't figure her friends out. Normally, they'd be happy to ride fifteen hours a day. *What* was going on?

"Well, then, I'll just ride by myself," she said, the annoyance clear in her voice. "Stewball and I will have a wonderful time!"

With that, she pushed back her chair, picked up her plates to clear, and strode out of the mess hall.

"I'm on wrapping!" Lisa announced as soon as the door closed behind Stevie. "I *love* to wrap."

"That's okay," Carole said. "I always get the paper bunched up at the corners. I'll finish the lanterns I was working on. What are you going to do?" she asked Kate.

"Mom and I have some planning to do on the cake and the rest of the barbecue. Let's get to work. Time's a-wastin'!"

12

AT FOUR-THIRTY the next morning, the four members of The Saddle Club awaited Christine's arrival. They would join Christine on her morning ride and end up at her house for breakfast. Their horses were in the corral. Each had a bridle, but no saddle. Christine was serious about bareback riding!

The girls had ridden bareback before. It was part of basic equestrian training to be able to ride bareback, but they all thought saddles were more comfortable. Still, bareback was the traditional Indian way and they were going for a ride with an Indian girl.

They waited in the quiet predawn darkness. Nobody spoke. The only sounds were those made by their horses. Berry whinnied. Stewball snorted.

"Riders up!" It was Christine. She and Arrow had

arrived so quietly that the girls hadn't even heard them approach.

"You're something," Stevie said admiringly.

"Old Indian trick," Christine said, pretending to speak like a Hollywood Indian.

"Give me a break," Kate teased. "The county just put fresh dirt on the road and graded it. *That's* how you snuck up on us!"

"Like I said," Christine joked, "old Indian trick! Come on, let's go."

The girls mounted their horses from the corral fence. It was tricky to get on a full-size horse without stirrups, but they found that they could climb on from the top of the fence.

In a few seconds, they were all ready to follow Christine. She led them across the range. Their eyes had become accustomed to the darkness. Although they couldn't always distinguish a bush from a rock, they could see well enough to navigate—and to follow Christine.

The air was still cool. Stevie could feel goose bumps rise, caused by the breeze that washed over her as Stewball trotted along comfortably. She rubbed her arm for warmth, then leaned toward the horse's mane, brushing his soft, warm coat.

One of the most important things Stevie had ever learned about riding—and it had taken her a long time to master it—was balance. A rider had to be careful to be centered on the horse, not too far forward or back, and most important, not to one side or the other. Learning balance had meant learning the horse's motion because the balance of the horse itself changed with each step as the horse's weight shifted from one foot to the next. What was a little tricky in a saddle was really tricky without one. Fortunately, all of the dudes were good enough riders to be able to manage bareback. In fact, after a short while, Stevie and the others got used to it.

"This is kind of neat," Lisa remarked, voicing what was on all of their minds. "I mean, Max is always telling me to feel the movement of the horse, but it's *hard* with a saddle. Now I can really feel the motion. It's easier to tell the paces and how they are different from one another. How do you think Max will like it when we want to take his horses out bareback?"

"I think he'll think we should have our heads examined," Carole said.

"It's not the head that can become damaged from riding without a saddle!" Christine teased. The girls all laughed. It was true that one of the other differences was the lack of cushion for the rider's backside.

"Now, come on up this way," Christine said. "It's a little tricky, though, so be careful."

The path turned out to be a narrow trail that snaked

around one of the hills on the range, rising gently most of the time. However, it had hairpin turns in it, and it was rocky all the way. They walked their horses very slowly so that the surefooted animals could pick their way.

Stevie was paying so much attention to the path that she didn't realize how breathtakingly beautiful the landscape was around her. When she arrived at the crest of the hill and Stewball drew to a halt next to Arrow, she looked up.

"Oh!" she gasped.

"I knew you'd understand," Christine said.

Stevie looked out over the range. From the top of the hill, in the dissipating darkness, she could see for miles in all directions. To the west, the sky was still dim, though the stars had disappeared and the moon was long set. To the east, however, the sun was cresting over the mountains that surrounded the valley, home of The Bar None, Two Mile Creek, and Christine's family. The sky was a brilliant mix of pinks, purples, and gold, boldly streaking the horizon.

"Look at that orange stripe!" Lisa said. "Isn't that something?"

"And the clouds that are pink, by the mountain peak there," Carole observed. "It looks just like cotton candy."

"Wait a minute, though, and all the colors will switch," Christine said.

While they watched, the sky brightened and the bold colors of dawn become pale pastels, and, finally, the deep blue of the daylight sky, streaked by high white wispy clouds.

"Look, there are our horses!" Kate said. The girls followed her gaze. The ranch's horses were in their pasture, perhaps two miles away, awakening for the day. They lifted their heads to see the dawn and then began munching contentedly on the sweet grass of the range.

"And there's the main house," Carole said.

"And our bunkhouse," Lisa added. "They look so small from here!"

"They even look smaller than *my* house," Christine said.

"Where *is* your house?" Stevie asked, suddenly very curious.

"Over that way," Christine said, pointing. "See, there's a small wood-frame house with an old barn attached. That's my home. Mom promised breakfast for us. We should get there just as the first griddle cakes go on the skillet."

"That's a great idea," Stevie said. "Because the next sound you're going to hear is the growling of my stomach. I can't believe how hungry I am these days!"

"Oh, yes I can," Christine said. "So let's get to it!"

Going down the hill turned out to be even trickier

than going up it. At least there was more daylight for the riders to see by so they managed okay. It just went slowly.

When they reached the flat part of the range, the girls first began trotting and then loping along, enjoying the freedom of the open countryside.

Stevie, Carole, and Lisa had never had more fun or felt more joyful on horseback. They were almost sorry when they pulled up to the Lonetrees' house.

Stevie hadn't known quite what to expect, but whatever it was, the Lonetree house wasn't it. They lived in a modern ranch house set near a hillside, with a creek cutting across their backyard. The barn, next to the main house, was home to Arrow and two other horses. There was a small paddock out back of the barn. The girls unbridled their horses and put them in the paddock. They also saw to it that there was plenty of cool water in the trough for the horses, and some fresh hay.

"Our turn!" Christine announced, once the horses had been taken care of.

The girls followed her into the house. It was very modern, decorated in a distinctly southwestern style. The floors were bare ceramic tile, and each of the rooms had tile set into the adobe walls. The tiles were decorated with Indian patterns. There was a big fireplace in the living room, which was also decorated with linen-covered chairs and a low coffee table, inlaid with more of the decorative tiles.

The kitchen, where they met Mrs. Lonetree, was completely modern, down to the microwave oven. Mrs. Lonetree greeted the girls with a warm smile and a handshake.

"I'm so glad to meet you all," she said. "Christine told me about how wonderful you were to her when Tomahawk died. I just want to thank you."

"Thank *us*?" Stevie asked, surprised. "Tomahawk saved my life. It's him we need to thank."

"Well, he was a wonderful dog," Mrs. Lonetree agreed. "Now, are you hungry? I hope so because I've made an awful lot of food for you."

"Starved," Carole said, speaking for all of them.

"Then have a seat."

The girls sat at the kitchen table, which had been set for them with beautiful earthenware plates.

"Where did you get these plates?" Stevie asked. "I've never seen anything like them."

"My mother made them," Christine told her friends proudly.

"You're a potter?" Lisa asked. "That's neat."

"Part-time," Mrs. Lonetree said. "Most of the time I'm a teacher. I teach modern European and Russian history at the Two Mile Creek High School. In the summertime, though, I usually have some extra time on my hands, so I throw pots—"

"Don't they break?" Stevie asked.

Christine stifled a giggle. "No, Stevie," she said. "Throwing pots is what potters do when they are working with wet clay on a potter's wheel. It's how they make things,"

"Oh," Stevie said sheepishly.

"See," Mrs. Lonetree explained, "working with clay is a traditional Indian craft. I learned most of what I know from my mother. I love the work I do and I love to use the traditional patterns of our people when I make pots. These things we keep at home. I also do a lot of urns and sort of primitive bowls. Those I sell at the tourist traps in town. A lot of the dudes like to think they've bought something made by an aged Indian woman working in the shade of her mud hut. They'd hate to see the high-quality work I can really do. They'd never pay for it!"

Stevie, Carole, and Lisa grinned at one another.

"Where's Dad?" Christine asked.

"He had to leave for work early this morning," Mrs. Lonetree explained.

"Dad's a research scientist," Christine told them. "He's always having to check on his experiments at odd hours."

Mrs. Lonetree served up the pancakes and sausages she'd prepared for the girls and they dug into them with relish. It was delicious, especially when they covered their pancakes with honey.

Stevie smiled to herself. A week earlier, she could never have imagined herself doing so many of the things she'd done in just the past few days, everything from going on a roundup, to riding bareback before dawn, to gobbling down pancakes in the home of a full-blooded American Indian. Life was full of surprises and a lot of them were pretty terrific, she concluded.

Christine said she wanted to show the girls something and excused herself for a few minutes. As soon as she was out of the room, Mrs. Lonetree leaned forward to speak to The Saddle Club in confidence.

"She's been heartbroken about Tomahawk, you know, but, of course, she doesn't blame you, Stevie. She knows these things happen. I'm trying to find a way to console her. I wanted to take her into town yesterday and see if we could buy her a pup from the breeder in town. Christine refused. I don't know what to do. Do you girls have any ideas?"

"I do," Carole said. Stevie knew that Carole understood Christine's loss better than any of them could since she'd lost the horse she'd loved the most in the world. His name had been Cobalt. "You can't *replace* an animal that's died any more than you can replace a person who has died. There's only one cure and that's time. In time, Christine will find that she *can* love another dog. But that other dog won't ever replace Tomahawk."

"You're very wise, Carole," Mrs. Lonetree said. "What I was trying to do was just that and it didn't work at all. I guess I just have to wait."

"Time will help," Carole said, her eyes growing dark and somber.

Christine reentered the room, bringing with her some of the trophies she had won in bareback-riding contests. She had fun describing the kinds of events she'd been in. The girls listened in rapt attention.

"I can't believe all the stuff I'm learning about horses on this trip," Stevie said. "And I thought I knew a lot before I got here."

"*That* was back when you were a dude!" Christine teased.

Stevie and the other girls laughed.

Then Kate pointed out that, speaking of dudes, it was time for all of them to head back to The Bar None. They thanked Mrs. Lonetree for the breakfast, and they especially thanked Christine for sharing her morning ride with them. It was a morning they would all remember for a long time to come.

"Hey, Christine," Kate said as they mounted their horses for the return trip. "We're having a picnic tomorrow at Parson's Rock. Want to come?"

"I'd love to," Christine said. "What time?"

"Come about noon," Kate told her.

"Can I bring something?" Christine asked.

"Just a sandwich for yourself," Kate said. "We'll be packing peanut butter and jelly. You know how it is."

"Yeah, I do," Christine said. "See you then."

Picnic? Tomorrow? Stevie thought in dismay. That was her birthday. Was she really going to have to eat peanut-butter-and-jelly sandwiches on her birthday, probably while Alex ate barbecued spareribs by the pool at home?

Stevie swallowed hard. It wasn't fair for her to expect a big deal for her birthday. She didn't want her friends to know she was upset. After all, it wasn't their fault that she'd miss her birthday.

13

"Isn't this pretty country?" Carole asked as the girls did their trail riding the next morning.

"Depends," Stevie grumbled. She and Stewball were riding right behind Berry. Lisa, on Chocolate, followed them.

"Depends on what?" Lisa asked.

"On how much you like circles," Stevie said. "I know you're in the lead, Carole, and the leader is the leader, but I swear we've passed this dead bush three times before."

"Hmmm, maybe you're right," Carole said.

And she continued in the same circle she'd been going in before.

Stevie didn't want to complain. She was in a bad mood anyway. It was her birthday and nobody had so much as wished her a happy birthday. Kate had disappeared after breakfast, saying something about peeling potatoes. It seemed to Stevie she'd heard an awful lot of talk about potatoes being peeled in the last couple of days. Something was going on and Stevie didn't like it.

Now, here she was, out in the middle of the range, with her two best friends, walking around in circles. In a little while, they were supposed to meet Kate and Christine at something called Parson's Rock to eat peanut-butter-and-jelly sandwiches. They didn't even have anything to drink with them. Kate had assured them there was a creek, "not far from the rock," whatever that meant. Considering how Stevie's day was going, "not far" probably meant about a quarter of a mile—a wonderful distance to walk when you had peanut butter stuck to your teeth.

She grimaced at the thought.

Lisa burst into song, singing something about "the tumbling tumbleweed." Lisa's singing was really getting to Stevie.

And today was their last full day at The Bar None. They would leave the next day before lunch to begin their long journey home. Two hours on the truck, three airplanes . . . Home suddenly seemed a very long way away. So did Alex, her twin brother, whose birthday she shared. She hated to admit it, but she was very homesick. Lisa's tumbling tumbleweed and Carole's big circles weren't helping. At all.

"There it is!" Carole said. "That must be Parson's Rock!"

"Of course it's Parson's Rock," Stevie grumbled. "It looks just like a pulpit and we know that because we've circled it about eight times!"

"Now, don't be mad at me," Carole said sweetly. "I just thought a nice quiet ride would be good for you. You seem sort of bummed today. Is something bothering you?"

"No," Stevie lied.

"I think the path is over here," Lisa said, gesturing to Carole. She led the way and they began the ascent to Parson's Rock.

Stevie's first suspicion that something was up came when she heard a roar of laughter. Christine and Kate were the only other people who were supposed to be there and Stevie didn't think they could laugh that loud.

Also, she swore she could smell the pungent odor of a barbecue fire, and something simply wonderful was being cooked on it. Maybe barbecued spareribs?

Then Stevie heard a series of "Shhhhs" that made her very suspicious. And as they rounded the final bend at Parson's Rock, Stevie spied the bright colors of decorations garlanding the trees.

"What's going on?" she asked her friends.

"SURPRISE!" was the answer as everybody from The Bar None jumped out from behind Parson's Rock to greet Stevie. She gaped at them in astonishment and understood the full impact only when she read the banner her friends had made for her. It read, HAPPY BIRTHDAY STEVIE (AND ALEX)!!!!!

"I don't believe this!" Stevie said, sliding down out of the saddle. "Is this really for me?"

"Is it somebody else's birthday?" Phyllis asked with a smile. "I hope not because then we've gone to an awful lot of trouble for the wrong person."

"No, there's no mistake," Stevie said. "It's my birthday. It really is. It's just that I didn't know anybody here had remembered it."

"Remembered it?" Carole asked. "Why, you must have told us about it twenty times *before* we left Virginia, and how many times since?" she asked Lisa.

Lisa shrugged. "Double digits, anyway," she teased. "We may be dumb dudes, Stevie, but we're not dumb. Anyway, there's nothing nicer than an excuse for a party."

"Especially if the party is a barbecue at Parson's Rock," Kate added.

"Ribs are almost ready," Frank announced. Phyllis and some of the guests hurried to set out the salads and the plates and the forks for their lunch.

Stevie's friends would have helped, too, but they were too busy getting hugs from her.

"You're the best friends a girl ever had," she said, hugging them all once again.

"Even if I sometimes just go around in circles?" Carole asked, laughing.

"I couldn't for the life of me figure out what you were doing," Stevie said. "I thought you'd gone crazy, but I wasn't ready to handle it, so I just let you wander around. Since I could tell we were circling this thing, I knew we weren't getting lost."

"Did you like my singing?" Lisa asked brightly.

"About as much as I liked Carole's circling," Stevie told her frankly. "Now, of course, I've changed my mind. I love every bit of it!"

"Good, because it's time for lunch. Your mother called Phyllis last week and gave her this barbecue recipe for ribs. I hope she got it right."

"I can tell just by the smell that she did," Stevie said, and when she'd had her first bite, she knew she was right.

Stevie could barely believe that all these people would go to so much work for her. She was really happy that Christine was there, and the Devines, of course. And she was glad that all the other guests from the ranch were joining in on her celebration. But the real surprise, and in a way the nicest one, was that Eli was there, too.

"Happy birthday, dude," he said, shyly offering his hand.

Stevie shook it gladly because she knew that she and Eli had become friends.

The food was just about perfect. Stevie couldn't believe that the Devines had actually managed to get a fully frosted birthday cake up to Parson's Rock. Phyllis was a wonderful cook and the cake tasted like the best Stevie had ever had.

She sat contentedly and quietly for a moment when she'd finished her second piece of birthday cake, surveying the party her friends had arranged for her. She liked being with her own family on her birthday, sure, but this was just great and she wouldn't have missed it for the world. She smiled to herself.

"Time for presents!" Carole announced.

Stevie couldn't believe it—presents, too?

When she saw the stack, she was even more astonished. "Why you guys must have brought four truckloads up here!"

"Five," Frank corrected her.

"Why do you think we had to be 'lost' for so long?" Carole asked.

Everybody laughed. "We watched you circling this

place," Kate said. "We thought you did a pretty good job of it. We timed the truck runs with your circles."

"What a terrific bunch of people you are," Stevie said. "I don't know how to thank you."

"You won't know *what* you're thanking us for until you open your presents," Christine reminded her.

Stevie picked up the first package, which was from Kate's parents. It was a red Western bandanna.

"Great, that'll keep the dust off my face on my next cattle drive—in Willow Creek," she said, slipping it up over her nose and mouth, cowboy-style. "Or maybe I'll rob a bank!"

The next was a present from The Saddle Club. Carole and Lisa had pitched in together to buy her a pair of beautiful black kidskin riding gloves.

"They're for your next show," Lisa said. "You'll be in dressage competitions soon, and you should have them."

Stevie smiled. They made her think of home, Pine Hollow Stables, and Comanche, her horse at the stable. She sniffed them. They had the wonderful rich smell of fine leather.

"They're perfect," she said, hugging her friends.

"And this is from me," Kate said, handing Stevie a very long package. Stevie opened it expectantly. It was a dressage whip, and it had been used many times.

"This is *yours?*" Stevie asked. Kate nodded. "You'd give me your very own riding whip?"

"I've hung up my spurs for English-riding competition," Kate reminded her. "You'll need it, and you'll use it well."

Kate had been a championship rider. Stevie knew it was a great honor for Kate to pass on her own riding whip to her.

"Thank you," she said, near tears.

"Come on, now, there are more gifts here to open," Frank said.

The other guests at the ranch gave Stevie nice gifts. She got a small bottle of cologne from one of the families, and a piece of primitive Indian pottery from the older couples. Stevie wondered if this was Mrs. Lonetree's work. She glanced at Christine, who shook her head ever so slightly. "It's beautiful," Stevie said.

There were two packages left. The first was small and square. The card said it was from Eli. Stevie opened it carefully, wondering what a wrangler would give a dude for a birthday present.

Inside the box was a tooled leather belt with an intricately decorated silver buckle, inlaid with turquoise.

She looked slyly at Eli. "Is this the kind of thing a dude would wear?" she asked him.

"No way," he said.

She stood up and removed the plain leather belt she

had on her jeans. She slipped her new one through and then buckled it snugly.

"It guess that means I'm not a dude anymore, huh?"

"Don't think you ever really were," Eli told her.

"That's the nicest thing you ever said to anybody, isn't it?" she teased him. He smiled at her. "Well, thank you, Eli. It's beautiful." She wanted to hug him, but she thought it would embarrass him, so she just shook his hand again. That seemed to embarrass him anyway.

Stevie reached for the final box. It was from Christine and it was very heavy. She lifted it carefully and untied the bow. When she'd taken the paper off, she opened the box. There was a lot of tissue paper. She removed it slowly.

When she was done unwrapping it, Stevie found herself holding a clay figurine of a German shepherd who was unmistakably Tomahawk. Stevie gasped softly.

"My mother made it," Christine said. "She made it last year. There are two of them. I have the other."

Stevie felt the tears well up in her eyes. She was sad, she was happy. She was overflowing with emotions. She had new friends, and old ones, and this seemed like the most wonderful day of her life.

"Oh, Christine!" she said, looking once again at the figurine Tomahawk. "It's perfect. Thank you!" She gave her new friend a very big hug, one that was long enough so that they could both control their tears before they parted and sat down.

Kate recognized that it was time to change the mood. "Eli," she said, handing him a rope, "would you show some of these Easterners some of the things you can do with a lariat?"

It only took a bit more urging to get Eli to show off. "This stuff's better on a horse," he said, but he did turn down offers to ride some of the horses who were at Parson's Rock. He showed the girls how to circle a lariat low and high, jumping in and out of the spinning rope like double-dutch. He then showed them how he could toss the loop onto small targets at great distances. He almost snagged a very surprised chipmunk.

It was a wonderful end to a wonderful party, Stevie thought, gazing at the pile of gifts at her feet.

14

"WHERE'D STEVIE GO?" Lisa asked Carole late that afternoon after they'd returned to The Bar None. They were with Kate in their bunkhouse, removing their riding clothes and donning bathing suits for a cool swim in the creek.

"Beats me," Carole said. "Do you know, Kate?"

"I saw her march off to the barn after Stewball was in the paddock, but I don't know what she was doing there. Maybe she just wanted to thank Eli again."

"Maybe," Lisa said. "But I thought Eli was done for the day after the horses were let out into the paddocks. Wouldn't he have gone to the wranglers' bunkhouse?"

"Oh, there's never any telling *where* Eli is," Kate said. "He's always full of surprises."

"And speaking of surprises," Lisa said, grinning

proudly. "We sure had one for Stevie today, didn't we? It was terrific. At least I thought so."

"I thought so, too," Stevie said, climbing up the steps of the bunkhouse. She'd heard their conversation through the open window. "It was an absolutely fabulous surprise. You had me totally fooled. I thought I was the only one in the world who remembered my birthday."

"You thought we were all deaf, dumb, and blind?" Carole asked. Stevie grinned. She had the feeling she was going to deserve what Carole was about to say to her. "You only mentioned it about forty-two times in the last few days. You must have thought we were pretty awful to be so coldhearted toward you."

"I did," Stevie said. "And I should have known you guys better! You did have a surprise for me. Surprises are so great. Both for the surpris*er* and the surpris*ee*." She smiled sagely, like a cat licking her chops after consuming a canary. Stevie sat down on her lower bunk and began yanking off her hot boots. She wiggled her toes. "Oh, that feels good. And the swim is going to feel even better."

"Wait a minute, there, Stevie," Kate said, holding her hand up in protest. "You were talking like you've got some kind of surprise planned. Do you know something we ought to know?"

Stevie feigned the most innocent look she could

manage. "Why, *whatever* could you be talking about?" she asked.

Carole, Lisa, and Kate suspected they wouldn't be able to get another word out of Stevie on the subject of surprises, but that didn't keep them from trying.

As the girls walked over to the swimming hole, towels over their shoulders, they pumped her for information. One by one, as they jumped into the crystal-clear waters, they pumped her. One by one, as they threatened to dunk her, they pumped her, but they didn't learn anything more useful. Stevie just kept on grinning happily. And, since she was a very good swimmer, she dunked them back.

THE NEXT MORNING, Stevie arose before her friends. They all had to get up early so they could be packed and ready to leave for the airport. As far as Stevie was concerned, that was a *terrible* reason to get up early. But Stevie had a better reason than that.

They'd made a date with Christine. They didn't have time to go for a dawn ride with her, but she'd agreed to come to their bunkhouse for a visit after she'd watched the sunrise and then join them all for a farewell breakfast of steak and eggs.

Stevie slipped out of her bunk and put on a clean pair of jeans, her new belt from Eli, a cowboy shirt, and her red bandanna. She decided she didn't care *how* out of place she'd look in the Washington airport, she wanted to wear her cowboy clothes.

When she was dressed, she left the bunkhouse, creeping silently into the gray dawn. She could see the first streaks of color coming over the mountains and she knew Christine would be there soon. She wanted to be ready.

She walked to the back of the barn and turned the knob on the cobweb-covered door, retracing her steps from her several visits to Mel and her puppies. This time, when she opened the final door to see the golden-colored mother and her puppies, Mel's tail wagged happily in greeting.

"I hope you don't mind," Stevie said. "I need to borrow one of your puppies for a while." Mel regarded her carefully. Stevie had the feeling that Mel knew she could trust her. "I'll take care of it," she promised. "And I'll bring it back."

Mel lay down and put her chin on her outstretched front paws. She watched every move Stevie made.

The puppies were waking up as the sun began filtering into their little room. It was a fact of life that all puppies were cute, Stevie thought. But which was the cutest?

The variety was astonishing. Some of them seemed to have more retriever blood than anything else. A couple of them looked like there was English sheepdog blood in them. Two tended toward a shepherd look. Stevie didn't think that was a good idea. And one had curly brown-and-white fur. His markings reminded Stevie of Stewball and she thought that was a good idea for what she had planned. She stroked the puppy's head gently as he slept. His eyes popped open and he stared at her for a second. Then, as if to thank her, he began licking her hand. His soft tongue tickled her skin. As he licked, Stevie could see that his hindquarters were going into action. In a flash, the little puppy was standing up because his tail was wagging so excitedly that he had to.

"I know a winner," she said, patting the puppy for a few more seconds. Then, while Mel watched dubiously, Stevie picked up her puppy. She gave the mother one more reassuring pat and left the room, closing the door carefully behind her.

In a few minutes, Stevie was back at the bunkhouse. During her absence, her friends had awakened to their alarm clock and had dressed as she had.

"Where have you been?" Carole asked.

"I've been working on my surprise," Stevie told her friends. And then, as she stepped up onto the porch, she produced the puppy.

"Where did *that* come from?" Carole asked, enchanted.

"It came from the barn," Stevie began to explain.

She sat down on the floor of the bunkhouse Indian-style to make a little pen for the puppy with her legs. She put him down gently and began playing with him as she explained. Her friends took turns patting the puppy, and having their hands licked, while Stevie talked.

"Eli has this dog, Mel," she began. "She had a litter of puppies and Eli wanted to keep it a secret so a whole bunch of dudes wouldn't bother the puppies too much. But they're almost old enough to be weaned now, and he wants to find homes for them."

"What on earth will your mother say?" Lisa asked, trying to think how she would explain it to her mother if she showed up with a puppy from a dude ranch.

"My mother?" Stevie said in surprise. "What's she got to do with it?"

"Aren't you planning to take him home?" Carole asked.

"Oh, no," Stevie said. "It's not for me. It's—"

There was the sound of steps on the bunkhouse porch. "Good morning!" Christine called to her friends. "You guys up now that the sun's already been up for a half an hour?" she teased.

And then all of The Saddle Club members understood what Stevie's surprise really was about.

"Come on in," Kate welcomed Christine. "We were just talking about you—or at least we were about to, weren't we, Stevie?"

Stevie nodded.

Christine opened the screen door and walked in. The four girls were sitting in a circle, surrounding a puppy who seemed intent on sniffing and exploring the entire universe in the next few moments.

"Oh, he's cute!" Christine said, leaning down between Carole and Lisa. "Whose is he?"

"He's Eli's now," Stevie said. "But he wants to find a good home for him. Tells me his mother's the finest herder he ever had. Don't know much about his father, though, but Eli thinks it's another herder."

"Eli knows good dogs, doesn't he?" Christine asked.

"Yes," Stevie said. "And I know good owners."

"Are you taking him back to Virginia with you?"

"Nope," Stevie said. "This dog belongs on the range. He belongs with horses and cattle. He doesn't look like much now—"

"Sure he does," Christine interrupted her. "He looks a *lot* like Stewball."

"My thought exactly," Stevie said. "See, we think alike." Christine laughed. "But I'm serious now," Stevie continued. "I'm always serious when it comes to animals and their owners."

Christine glanced at Stevie curiously. The puppy loped over to greet the newest arrival. Christine squatted down and automatically reached out to pat him. He automatically began licking her hand. When Christine picked him up, he began licking her neck.

She giggled from the tickling and fell over backward. The puppy started nibbling at her earlobes. Christine, who was normally quite reserved, couldn't stop laughing—or patting the puppy.

"See," Stevie said. "You've got to have him."

Christine's smile disappeared. "Stevie, I can't replace Tomahawk. No dog could replace him for me. I know you feel responsible, but you shouldn't. It wasn't your fault. It was a rattlesnake. They live here. Sometimes they kill dogs."

"I know," Stevie said. "I understand that now, though it wasn't easy for me to realize it. I also know that you can't replace Tomahawk. No dog can replace Tomahawk. He was one of a kind. But this little guy— well, he's one of another kind. Seems to me that he's another kind of dog you ought to have."

Christine removed the puppy's paws from her shoulder and lifted him into her lap. She patted his head and scratched him behind the ears as she spoke. "You could be right," she began, "but I'm not sure I can decide."

"I'm not sure it's you who's doing the deciding here," Stevie said sensibly. "Looks to me like it's already been done."

She pointed to the puppy who, exhausted from his exploring, tail wagging, and licking, had suddenly fallen sound asleep on Christine's legs.

"Oh," Christine said, as the puppy sighed contentedly. Then she smiled. "I guess it is decided." She hugged her new puppy very gently, so as not to wake him.

Then, while the puppy slept, the girls returned him to his mother. Eli had told Stevie they'd all be ready to leave Mel and go to their own homes in one week. Christine could have her pick of the litter, but it was clear that Stevie and the puppy had made the choice for her. They put the sleeping puppy down next to his mother. He snuggled up to Mel and then, still half-asleep, began nursing. Mel licked him.

The girls left the mother and her puppies, tiptoeing out of the room. It was time for their breakfast. It was time to finish packing. It was almost time to go.

"I've got it!" Christine announced at the breakfast table as she ate her steak.

"What have you got?" Stevie asked her.

"I've got the puppy's name," Christine told them all. They looked at her expectantly. "His name is Dude," she announced. "And every time I call him, I'll think of you all. That'll be great!"

Stevie and her friends thought so, too.

15

"WHERE ARE WE now?" Lisa asked Carole wearily. "I keep losing track." The three girls were sitting in a row of identical chrome-and-plastic chairs in an airport that looked very much like the previous two they'd been in—only bigger.

"We're in Denver," Carole said. "Stapleton Airport, it's called. We just have one more flight and it's going to leave in a half an hour from that gate there." She pointed to a desk where they had already checked in for their flight. "Until then, we wait."

"I don't know about you guys, but I had a great time at The Bar None Ranch."

"Me, too," Carole said.

"Especially me," Stevie added. "It hardly seems possible that only a week ago, we'd never ridden Western, never herded cattle, never met Christine or Eli. Now it all seems familiar, and they seem like good friends."

"Is it going to be hard going back to *English* riding?" Lisa wondered out loud.

"I don't think so," Carole said. "After all, if we learned anything from our Western riding experience, it's that horses are horses and the kind of saddle you put on them doesn't change that. But don't forget to post when you trot."

"Max'll see to that!"

There was a click and the public-address system came to life, announcing that they were boarding all passengers bound for Washington, D.C. The girls picked up their hand luggage and headed for the gate, filing quietly onto the plane. Stevie couldn't help feeling that every airplane was taking her farther away from The Bar None—in more ways than one. Of course, each plane took them more miles from the ranch and their friends, but on each plane, there were fewer and fewer passengers dressed in Western clothes. There were fewer people around them who talked the way Eli liked to drawl. It was as if the trip itself were a way for them to make the long and difficult transition from ranch life to suburban Virginia.

The girls settled into their seats, three in a row,

buckled their seat belts, put their tray tables and seat backs into their full upright and locked positions in preparation for takeoff, and started talking again.

"The Saddle Club's split up, now," Stevie said glumly. "Kate's way out west. We're in the east."

"Kate is the Western division of The Saddle Club," Carole said. "We are the Virginia branch."

Stevie grinned and thought that was an interesting way to look at it.

The three girls were all lost in their own thoughts as the plane began to taxi down the runway. Shortly after takeoff, flight attendants began to pass out sodas and snacks.

"You know," Lisa said as she ripped open her bag of nuts, "I've been thinking about what Carole said before." Both Carole and Stevie looked at her. "To me, The Saddle Club is what we are, who we are, wherever we are. Being together is nice, but just being The Saddle Club is nice, too. It's not as if we're split up by a measly couple of thousand miles. It's that we're joined by a common interest, a common bond. We're us. We're The Saddle Club."

Stevie looked at Lisa and smiled. "That's a pretty neat way to look at it," she said. "You just might be right, too."

"Lisa's given me an idea," Carole said. "Why don't

we try to make The Saddle Club a worldwide opera-
tion? Everywhere we go, we'll try to start new groups!"

"You planning to do a lot of traveling?" Stevie asked
Carole. "International branches in London and
Amsterdam and all that? Maybe even Sydney?"

Carole smiled sheepishly. "I guess I've gotten a bit
ahead of myself," she admitted. "For now, I think *two*
branches are just fine. And Lisa's right, The Saddle
Club *is* wherever we are."

"I'll drink to that," Stevie quipped as she twisted
open a bottle of soda. They clinked their plastic glasses
together.

"One thing, though," Stevie said. "I think that
maybe we should get at least one more Saddle Club
pin." She glanced down at the silver horse head on her
shirt collar. "And I think that the next time we go to
The Bar None, we should give it to Christine."

"That's a *wonderful* idea!" Carole said as the three
girls clinked their glasses again.

And as they did it, each thought that it was hard to
tell which was the *better* part of the idea: having Christine join The Saddle Club, or returning to The Bar
None.

It didn't matter. They were *both* great ideas.

ABOUT THE AUTHOR

Bonnie Bryant is the author of nearly a hundred books about horses, including The Saddle Club series, Saddle Club Super Editions, and the Pony Tails series. She has also written novels and movie novelizations under her married name, B. B. Hiller.

Ms. Bryant began writing The Saddle Club in 1986. Although she had done some riding before that, she intensified her studies then and found herself learning right along with her characters Stevie, Carole, and Lisa. She claims that they are all much better riders than she is.

Ms. Bryant was born and raised in New York City. She still lives there, in Greenwich Village, with her two sons.